Rare Air

Lessons from the Crisis of an Inconvenient Woman

Rowin Kaci Clese

BTA Consulting LLC—Lakewood, OH
ISBN: 979-8218133603
Library of Congress Control Number: 2023900841
Title: *Rare Air: Lessons from the Crisis of an Inconvenient Woman*
Author: Rowin Kaci Clese
Digital distribution | 2022
Paperback | 2022

This is a work of fiction. The characters, names, incidents, places, and dialogue are products of the author's imagination, and are not to be construed as real.

Dedication

iii

To the members of the Female Disruptor Posse (The FDP). All of you...because of you. I humbly thank you on the other side.

Table of Contents

Prologue

It doesn't happen often. It has never happened to her even once that she can recall. Think about it: you're in a crisis- a crisis of such professional or personal significance that you are auto-piloting between self-preservation, defensive maneuvers and what can only be likened to moments of pure chaos. Your new normal is shifting sands beneath your feet that you've learned to dance over with what you hope resembles grace. You've gotten so good at answering the how-are-yous and what-have-you-been-up-tos that you don't have to think about it anymore. You don't eat like you used to or sleep nearly as much as you should, but your body has adjusted. You've adjusted. You've now dealt with this *thing* much longer than you ever thought possible. It's literally part of who you are now. Your crisis.

Then it happens. Time stops. Life stops. You stop.

Suddenly you have time to think and to breathe and to sleep. Oh, glorious sleep. The crisis-your crisis-is still very much alive and well, but you...you now have *space*. Space that you haven't had. Space that you forgot you needed. It's so foreign and weird that during the first few days you almost have a panic attack because of the novel calm that's come over your world. You have time to reflect on your crisis while it's still ongoing rather than on the other side of it like some war-torn skeleton of yourself. Your retrospective wouldas and couldas now have the chance to be Should-I's and Will-I's. This is incredible.

Yeah…*this* never happens.

That is, until it did to her…that day.

This is the story of Anslie Krewicco. She could be you. In the Spring of 2020, smack dab in the middle of her crisis and only days before the United States began initiating shelter-in-place orders due to COVID-19, she was forced on administrative leave (more on that later). Suddenly, after two years of her now not-so-new fucked up normal, everything stopped. And by "everything," let's face it…everything stood still immediately. Think about it. Sure, her world of work certainly came to a halt: no clients, no weekly business travel across the country, no meetings, no emails, no check-in calls. But the immediate world around her also stopped simultaneously: restaurants and various stores closed, parks became desolate, grocery stores became empty due to people hoarding supplies quicker than stores could get them restocked and everyone was strongly encouraged to just stay home. In other words, her fucked up normal just got one-upped. For any of you who were dealing with something "big" at that time, you remember…it skipped right over "huge" and landed in the "you've got to be fucking kidding me" category. Anslie was right there with you.

During the first few weeks of being wholly unsupervised, despite recognizing the severity of the pandemic that was upon us, Anslie enjoyed the hell out of herself. She had a historic home that she was actually getting to work on and enjoy. Her dogs had a fur mom rather than this random woman who slept in the house on the few nights that the dog sitter wasn't home. She gardened and worked out every day. She chitchatted with neighbors. She read books that she had never finished. And she started doing a bunch of little craft projects like making candles and wind chimes…who knew that she even wanted to do that? Well, the new Type A Hippie Anslie did, that's for sure.

And then one day in mid-April while she was tending to her crisis…because remember it is still alive and kicking…something hit her: You are breathing very rare air, sister.

The universe had momentarily worked out in such a way that she had been gifted with as much uninterrupted time and space as she wanted to deal with her crisis *now…. while it is happening*. Take a minute to let that soak in. Not only was she not killing herself to succeed and act professional while contending with the cast of bad actors in her crisis, but she also couldn't really go anywhere or do anything that would subconsciously, or even deliberately, distract her. She could, for all practical purposes, just be still to think, to feel, to weigh options, to plan, to…what-the-hell-ever. At 45, nothing like this had ever happened to her before and she was pretty sure in that moment that it would never happen again. Now, at nearly 5 months in this, her *new* normal, she is absolutely certain that it will never happen again.

What's a girl to do with such a profound personal epiphany and with all this time? Well, Anslie decided to start writing.

Writing about her navigation through the last two years of what often resembled a Dateline Special. Writing about the reflections and questions of the last few months. Writing about her new forms of crisis management. Writing about what her dogs taught her about talking to attorneys. Writing about this amazing, rare air. Following is her story in her own words…

Chapter 1
Pit of Despair

Let me start by saying that I am in no way a counselor or a therapist or some other medical person who has conducted clinical studies on human behavior. I am a businesswoman. I'm known to be excellent at what I do. I'm known to be objective, resourceful, analytical, diligent, and thoughtful. Someone who speaks truth to power. I'm also known in some circles to be stubborn, not a team player, directive, too strong, difficult, and defiant. My "studies" are leading initiatives in a very male-dominated professional field and herding the cats needed to bring those initiatives to fruition. If I do my thing correctly, people ultimately get better service and have better outcomes from using them. Companies ultimately either save or make more money and decrease inefficiencies. Sounds good, right? Only problem is that all those wonderful, utopic things require people to change and no matter how phenomenal the results sound, people hate change. People hear *change* and people hear *what I've been doing is wrong*. And, in the professional environment where I reside, they often hear *this woman is telling me what I've been doing is wrong*. Hence, the variety of self-descriptors I shared above.

Like thousands of other women in the business world, I work in a systemically misogynistic environment. Mind you, not the blatant, in-your-face, sweetheart-you-have-a-nice-ass, dark oak conference room, cigars, and strip clubs of old misogyny, but rather the modern, dog whistle, don't-be-so-emotional, she's-ambitious, you-need-a-few-more-leadership-opportunities-for-us-to-promote-you shiny, new misogyny. Don't get me wrong—the blatant old schoolers are still creeping around our hallways and meetings, but they have been overshadowed by their beguiling newbie counterparts and those counterparts are running much of the show, and doing it quite smoothly, I might add. My company has female leaders who have won those female industry leader-type awards. My company touts donating time, money, and energies to supporting and developing women. My company brings in eloquent female keynote speakers to events and forges new paths in helping women with a variety of disease states. My company portrays the optics of a female empowering mecca from the outside.

From the outside.

I joined a new business unit within the organization a little over 4 years ago. I was excited for the breath of fresh air and to learn about an industry space I had not previously experienced. I would be traveling quite a bit more than I had in recent years, but I wasn't worried. I had done the road warrior thing before. The pace was going to be quick. The expectations high. This was my wheelhouse.

However, within what felt like a minute, but was actually about 90 days, I learned that things were going to be very different in this wheelhouse.

As a requirement, I went to the mothership for a 2-week crash course in my new world. Once settled at my hotel, I decided to meet up with a couple of classmates for a bite to eat. While waiting for them, my phone rings and I see it is my new management partner, Hayden (you will get to know Hayden extensively through this book). Hayden called to let me know that there was something she just had to tell me and, after downing 2 martinis, she had mustered up the courage to do so. What fresh hell could this be?

Seems as though Hayden was chatting with one of her closest friends and one of my immediate colleagues, Evan, where he shared that he was recently at a client dinner with our director, Stanley. According to Evan, when the clients, who would ultimately be my direct responsibility, asked Stanley about this new woman he just hired, Stanley eloquently responded, "She wears a skirt and is a lot better looking than Evan. You'll really like her." Fucking fantastic.

As slightly tipsy Hayden was going on and on about my situation that had somehow become about her, only 2 things went through my mind on the eve of my formal training: one, why did she seem almost excited to be telling me about my boss's sexist behavior? And two, if this sort of behavior was okay to do with clients and then ok to discuss between employees, where on earth was the bar for what was not ok?

Next up on the docket almost back-to-back was a national conference where we would be meeting with key opinion leaders from around the country, soon followed by a management meeting in Chicago. The society conference was as you would expect: people drinking way too much, people forgetting they were married, people trying to influence others to attend their corporate event or order their legacy products or buy their next greatest thing. But what floored me was how brazen everyone was about, well, everything. One case in point was a dinner I was asked to attend. Twenty or so people dining on a beautiful restaurant's patio, a few of my colleagues were there and it was a relatively early 8 pm. Across from me was one of our female sales reps and to the left of me was one of her clients. For the better part of an hour and a half, the sales rep not only watched me deflect her client's advances, but she also encouraged him to continue doing so, laughing and oh-you're-so-sillying him along the way. He was a delightful combo of drinking too much and forgetting he was married. I was a lucky gal. When the breaking point finally hit of him grabbing my leg under the table, I stood up and walked out. The sales rep gave me this pained, appalled look that only made me shake my head in disbelief. When I stopped at the other end of the table to tell my male colleague that I was leaving, and more importantly why I was leaving, he shared with me that the sales rep was probably excited that the customer was engaged because he was difficult for her to access. Are you kidding me? Sorry, pal, I'm not a party favor for Mr. Hard-To-See.

The saddest part about that dinner was that it was only one of the many sexist situations that occurred at the conference…all of which were seemingly endorsed, or at least condoned, by men AND women at my company. I immediately reverted to hearing what I thought was some kind of weird excitement or eagerness in Hayden's voice that night she called me a few weeks prior. What was going on? Had I entered some strange group where objectifying women had gone from expected to accepted, to now it's some kind of compliment to women? Jesus. And where was that What's-Not-Ok bar?

I was still wrestling with what my new normal really was when the management meeting popped up about a week later. My first official meeting with the other leaders of my new business unit. There were not a lot of women but the ones that were there were seemed to pack a punch. In fact, the head of the business unit was a woman so certainly this should bring some light into my new normal. I was so excited to get started that I powered through a legitimate, find-some-Pedialyte, bought of food poisoning to make it to breakfast that first morning. Everyone would be there—sales, marketing, operational leaders. This new girl had to show up.

Sure enough when I got to the breakfast area, there was a huge round table where all of these people were chatting away about the places they checked out downtown the night before, eating their eggs and drinking their coffees. Laughing. There was lots of laughing. This will be good, I thought. Totally worth crawling off the hotel bathroom floor and downing that Pedialyte.

As I approached the table it was a pretty snug fit, so I tried to guess how and where best to sit. As I scanned the table, an operational leader, Jack, looked up at me and immediately started making room for me to sit. As he was shuffling around, I was saying hi to some, introducing myself to others. He pulled out my chair and when he did, I noticed he left his arm on the back of it. Ok, that's weird, but I'm here with maybe 15 people. Shit, the FEMALE HEAD OF THE BUSINESS UNIT is here. This will be fine.

And then, just as I was realizing he still hadn't moved his arm and now was leaning in terribly close for a casual, get-to-know-you, business conversation…just as my Spidey senses were kicking in…the female department head loudly laughs from across the table, "Hey, Jack, maybe give Anslie a minute…this is her first meeting. Just try to be a little less *you*, ok?" The table immediately started laughing and I heard comments about "easing her into how Jack is." What. The. Fuck.

So, let's recap: in less than 90 days my new boss has basically described me as nothing but eye candy, I was used as bait with a difficult client, and now this breakfast scenario that I don't even know how to describe happened. Yeah, that What's-Not-Ok bar was galaxies away from where I sat.

As any woman that reads this knows, the encounters I just described are bad, but they're not even near the realm of horrific (don't worry…we'll get there, too). Sure, they *are* bad. They suck. You might speak up and say something. You'll definitely tell your girlfriends about it over a cocktail when you get home. But you're certainly not leaving a new job because of any of these things just like you didn't leave any jobs before when similar shit happened to you. You're certainly not in a pit of despair. But you have suddenly become keenly aware that if you're not careful, you could end up in one and you're looking at the people who could very well put you there.

As we get to know each other through the chapters in this book, you'll see me reference many other, far more egregious misogynistic acts. Ones that caused me to stand up, to shout, to name names and take numbers. Ones that caused me to be a royal pain in the ass to the new modern misogynists and their followers. Ones that put the eventual target on my back. But for now, let's jump into the pit of despair that eventually caused me to be breathing this amazing, rare air.

Earlier I introduced you to Hayden, Evan and Stanley. Let's do a quick regroup and refocus here of our cast members. Hayden is my direct sales management partner. Every Sales Manager is partnered with someone like me in the workflow-analytics-nerd space, and then they collectively support a region of sales reps. Pretty straightforward. Evan, originally in a role like myself, got promoted to National Director (more about that later), making him now Hayden's boss and Stanley's peer/partner. Rumors about Hayden and Evan having a less-than-professional relationship have been swirling for years, so there's that, too…made even more interesting now by their new working relationship. And Stanley, my current boss and Evan's previous boss, was an Associate Director of the Nerds for maybe 5 years and then around the time Evan got promoted, Stanley also mysteriously was promoted to National Director of his realm. A lot of mysterious, weird, and generally fucked up things began happening around this time. It was late summer/early fall a few years ago at this point and, unbeknownst to me, the momentum of my crisis was quietly beginning to build in the shadows.

During that time, one of Hayden's sales reps, Mimi, called me ecstatic on a Wednesday afternoon. I remember it so clearly because of how rare it was for Mimi to be calling me with such high positive energy. Sure, she called a lot. I mean a lot. And there was always tons of energy behind those calls, or the 16 text messages I would receive immediately if I didn't answer the phone. But mostly those communications were for some perceived wrong or injustice committed by a customer or the company unto her that was hindering her ability to sell or achieve or whatever in the hell she wanted to do but wasn't allowed. This call was different.

She had a solution for one of our never-satisfied, always-wanting-more key clients. And she didn't have just any solution. She had a revenue-generating solution that had already been proven to work in another key client's office. Who? What? Where? Tell me more. I jumped right on the Mimi train. Choo Choo.

It then went something like this:

Mimi tells me the plan.

I tell her it's illegal.

Mimi tells me it can't be illegal because Hayden and Evan have had this plan set up for months in another location.

I tell her it's illegal.

Mimi says her and Hayden are going to present the idea to the key client.

I tell her it's illegal…and not to talk to anybody…I need to talk to Hayden first.

Mimi is none too pleased that I not only got off her train, but I derailed it on my deboard.

See, in the highly regulated, manufacturing industry I supported, for as many hazy shades of gray that people hear about on the national news or in their Yahoo feed, there are just as many clear cut, black and white things employees can and cannot do. One of those definite no-no's is directly financially incentivizing industry leaders and professionals to use a company's products. Granted, companies find all sorts of ways around that, though, through speaker bureaus and rebates and "supporting this or that fundraiser walk." But you definitely can't say, for instance, "Hey, Bob, for every widget you order, we'll give you $50." In that same vein, manufacturing vendor and supplies employees in my industry can't recommend to a client that they start charging their customers for new and improved services that either don't exist or are provided to them for free by the vendor. And it's an even bigger no-no if enabling the client to charge or mislead their customers in such a way directly generates kick-back revenue for the company providing the FREE service.

That was the plan.

Hence, my dramatic jump off the Mimi train.

Over the course of the next week or so, I reached out to Hayden not once, but twice to clarify the situation. I was hoping that human nature was firmly on my side and that Mimi had misheard or misinterpreted what Hayden said, likely morphing the real innocuous scenario into this crazy story because it's this crazy story that would make her a savior to the difficult key client. I talked to Hayden for almost 2 hours total. Nope. No embellishment. No linguistic liberties. Shit happened just as Mimi described.

I decided to further verify my beliefs before going to Stanley and his boss, so I contacted a person who I trusted that was far more in-the-know about the free service in question than I was. Yep. Illegal. Zero nuances there. That verification triggered me requesting an emergency call the next morning with Stanley and his boss. Wait…we haven't named Stanley's boss yet…let's go with Don.

By happenstance, both Stanley and Don were attending the same meeting, making getting them on a call a smidge easier. I grabbed 15 minutes of their time before their day officially got started. I bullet pointed what had happened, what I knew about this subject matter based on a previous vendor sales role I held, and what I feared the consequences could be for the company. This free service Mimi was monetizing for the client was directly tied to several million dollars in incremental annual revenue for our company so we should want to protect its integrity and purpose. To sweeten their willingness to act I even gave Hayden and Evan an out: I was certain it was an innocent mistake based on trying to please a customer rather than deliberately doing something that was fraudulent. Shit, since it was likely Stanley or Don who approved the plan, I even included the phrase "anyone that was involved in the project was probably well-intended." No dice. They hung up without so much as even a hint of concern or thanks for the heads up.

What I didn't know then, but what I realize now, is that you rarely know peoples' true end games in any given situation, let alone a precarious situation (we'll discuss that more later in, you guessed it, the "End Games" chapter). Even if your emotional intelligence is through the roof. Even if you find a politically correct way to ask them or you gather some intel on the other people, you're still unlikely to know…mainly because it's unlikely that the other person even truly knows their end game in that moment. Sure, they can probably muster up something to do with reputation or "the truth" or "what's best for the company," but those are all umbrellas. Easily spoken shields to protect the real end game: I don't want anything bad to happen to me…*ever*. And this situation that I was trying to rectify had bad written all over it for everyone I was talking to or talking about.

Over the next 4 weeks, that weird, mysterious stuff I alluded to earlier started to happen. My repeated inquiries to Stanley about what Legal or Compliance had to say about my findings were dismissed. A couple of vague, blanket emails about "business code of conduct" were sent out as non-answer answers to my questions. On the other hand, Stanley started questioning me about the most trivial aspects of my work from meals during business travel to wanting cc'd on emails to long-term clients to how I was communicating with my sales reps. Hayden started only communicating with me on an as-needed, often negative, or accusatory toned basis. Oh, and like a weird set of dominoes falling in a matter of weeks, the GM of the business unit got promoted to President of a bigger business unit. Don got promoted to GM. Stanley got promoted to National Director. And Evan got promoted to National Director. How's that for an end game strategy?

But as you might have guessed, those promotions weren't the end to their end game. They still had one problem that those promotions and salary increases didn't fix…me.

What transpired from the Fall of that year pretty much up until I was forced onto administrative leave in the Spring of 2020 is difficult to comprehend, even for me now. I think about events and moments more often than I care to admit and at times I still feel overwhelmed even though those times have passed. Like I said at the beginning, *this thing* becomes a part of you.

See, since they had no grounds for firing a top performer who carried a larger book of business than all of her peers, this like-minded cast of characters had to find one. And, if that failed, well, they'd just have to move hell and high water to create one.

It all started petty enough that Fall: questioning me here, insisting I do extra work there. Things that were only truly noticeable to me. Things that if I complained or pushed back could be chalked up to either me misinterpreting interactions, or better yet, that I simply didn't want to do my job. You know what I'm talking about…some good old-fashioned gaslighting. After several weeks of needling behaviors not having the impact that they wanted, it's as though a collective agreement was then made that it was time to up the ante.

They drew ire and fault in an inclusive professional group I developed for clients to give them a voice in a field where they often felt muffled, claiming among other things that in not inviting my business unit leaders to attend or address the group I was deliberately being exclusive to my business leaders. They fabricated a 30-point corrective action plan, allegedly based on one questionable communication, that resulted in 28 pre-selected employees, many who I learned later were coached, submitting 360 reviews on my behavior and my entire body of work being questioned. A complicit HR department interviewed employees about my character and then admitted to me later they knew the accusations were false, but that I should "just keep my head down and get through it." They removed key accounts from my responsibilities, decreasing my potential earnings. They dismissed several live conversations I had with multiple Compliance Officers, an HR Director, an HR Senior Manager and Divisional Presidents where I reiterated the fraudulent situation I uncovered and the subsequent retaliation and harassment to me that ensued. They changed a compensation plan with only weeks left in the fiscal year that only impacted my earnings and awards. They enlisted unsuspecting, young sales reps by acting as confidantes to listen to their woes and help them with their career but then filed anything that was said about me by them with HR. After I finally filed an EEOC complaint more than a year later, they came after my friends, auditing emails and expense reports from months passed because in the words of one Compliance Officer to a friend of mine when she asked, "Are they coming after Anslie's friends because they can't go after her anymore since she filed with the EEOC?"

"Well, what I can say is that you should watch your back," as he stared unblinking back at her.

Stanley publicly shared, erroneously on top of it, information from my mid-year review with peers and subordinates. Hayden sent diatribes of emails to me and about me, cc'ing our leadership, on wrongs I either didn't know existed or that she believed I would inevitably commit. It was incessant. They came. And they came again and again, even after the EEOC became involved. Even after they knew I had legal counsel. Even after they continued to dig into my life and my work and my friends, only to find nothing damning against me. In retrospect, it was incredible, really. I would even go so far as to say their efforts were prolific.

But here's the thing…and during these last couple of years I've had this conversation more times than I can count with the small handful of people in my trust tree…I don't know if it's these bad actors' arrogance or stupidity that has caused them to perpetuate this chaos, this crisis of mine. I suspect that its some combination of both where the ratio fluctuates dependent on the day and topic and likely the amount of angst caused by their latest ill-fated attempt at my demise. But, if you knew me, and they do know me quite well professionally, you would never go up against me on a situation that I am passionate about or where my integrity is on the line-and this situation is both. It combines overcharging and misleading customers across the country, treating others with less than equality and respect, and striving without limitations to destroy my reputation and career all in an effort to protect those of bad actors. Yeah, if I were them, I would have found something else to do. Pretty much anything else to do.

When I try to imagine myself in these peoples' shoes, I am left to wonder why no one has ever taken a step back to ask some very basic questions. As weeks turned into months and months turned into years: Why in the hell *is* Anslie so confident that she can see this situation through? We have buried the fraud and we have burned her for bringing it to light. Why hasn't she crumbled yet? And furthermore, how is she even still here, let alone succeeding as she is?

If anyone in that group of people had paused for a moment…just a single moment over these last 2 years…and seriously contemplated those questions, I really think they might have stopped. I think some things might have been fixed or addressed because I think they would have realized that I was most likely approaching this insane, disparaging situation the same way I approached my work:

With unwavering focus, belief in myself, tireless efforts, and that integrity I just mentioned. And I was very unlikely to stop.

And as that realization sunk in, I believe they then might have nervously wondered, if I was, in fact, approaching this situation like my work: How was Anslie following up and with who? If Anslie wasn't retaliating against the cast of bad actors or defiantly blowing off her responsibilities, what was she doing with all of the information from conversations and emails and meetings? Who was she actually talking to and what was her motivation? Or, in the words of Chris Voss, author of *Never Split the Difference*, what was her "Black Swan?"

But because they never really thought about why I was still in the fight, they also didn't stop to think about much else that tends to go along with unwavering focus, belief in oneself, tireless efforts, and integrity: that given the circumstances, I was probably documenting and recording conversations, printing every email before they could disappear and maintaining real-time notes on every last interaction, instance and infraction that occurred. Or, that my attorney who is affiliated with the #MeToo Organization, the EEOC investigators and my company's attorneys were going to have complete access to all of it.

I guess that takes care of that confidence question.

And I suppose that it also might help you understand a little bit about how at the same time I was projecting such confidence, I ended up in a personal pit of despair. Rest assured; I was self-instructing a master class in compartmentalization. And while the skill served me well, it came at a high cost to my mental, physical, and emotional health. Everything that you can think of happened from not sleeping or eating and having panic attacks, to things you probably cannot even imagine happening like waking up every morning with parts of your hairline having turned white from stress overnight and making sure you never walked anywhere alone at corporate events for years so that you could at best avoid being ambushed, but at least would have a witness if you were. It was so gut-wrenching and heartbreaking at times that I would be in whatever city curled up in a ball in whatever hotel I was in that night with tears simply running down my face, unable to even call a friend for support. Some of the most branded moments in my mind, however, were not on the days where horrific things happened to me, I had learned to compartmentalize those moments with expertise. But rather, the days that my friends' lives were impacted *because of me*…those were devastating. Debilitating. And, as many of you who have stood up or stood alone for something know, you are never the only one and you are rarely the one who has had the worst of it. But once you have been standing in your truth for a while, however quietly or loudly that may be, others who have not yet come forward do come to you. What I learned experience after experience that had either been reported and dismissed, or never reported because they knew it would be dismissed, was that I wasn't just in the fight for me anymore. I wasn't alone in this pit of despair…I was just its newest most vocal member.

So here I find myself now, breathing this *rare air*. Figuring out how to embrace this pause in the universe while taking stock in what I have done and haven't done, what I've thought and felt…and how my reactions to other peoples' actions have impacted me and at times inspired others.

So often after I've either had to restate some terrible event for the tenth time or type information for some legal document for my attorney or been faced with the latest attempted mindfuck, I've sat back with one of those heavy-sounding mouth breaths and wondered out loud to myself, "Are you really ok?

Because based on this shit, you shouldn't be ok. In fact, you should be very much not ok." But then here I am…still sharing a bunk and spooning with my crisis, but no longer in the pit of despair. And this may sound too simplistic to some, but the first step out, the first reach up and out of that pit, was that heavy sounding, emptying breath…and figuring out what power and strength could come from it.

Chapter 2
Breathe Through

Follow your breath. Let your breath guide your movements. Just breathe. We could be on a yoga mat in any yoga studio anywhere. It's all about the breath. It's all about listening to your body. Just breathe.

Years ago I began dabbling in yoga, mostly because as a multi-sporter I was a horrible stretcher, causing me to be prone to completely avoidable injuries…if only I would stretch more. I could just never consistently commit to it. Working out regularly? Absolutely. Taking an extra 10 minutes so that I could keep working out regularly? Not a chance.

I figured going every so often to an hour-long class that was all about stretching couldn't hurt. I probably even rationalized going to one class would equate to stretching appropriately for 10 minutes after 6 different workouts. The mind has a funny way of helping you avoid things you don't want to do in the first place.

One part of my initial yoga experiences that I both struggled with and embraced was the breathing. As a distance runner by nature, I embraced it. I understood the benefits of rhythmic, controlled breathing. Breathing could make or break a good run. If I maintained it, I felt like I was gliding across the pavement and could run for miles. If I didn't? I could feel my heart beating out of my chest while I was panting out what I was certain were my last breaths on earth.

But allowing my breathing to control my movements? That didn't make much sense to me. I mean, how could an inhale help me lift my arm, or an exhale help me do a sit up? My muscles did those things. My muscles helped me run and bike and lift weights and hike and tackle obstacles in those races that have become so popular over the last decade…not my breath.

Oddly enough it wasn't until the last couple of years, though, that I realized just how wrong my thinking about the strength of breath was. That my muscles may have *allowed* me to do a lot of physical things, but it was my breath that gave me the actual *strength* to do them. To keep moving when I was just too exhausted to stand. To stay calm and focused when emotional kidnappers were trying to shove me into their van. And to hold on when I felt like I was falling.

Near the end of 2018, I was attending an industry conference in Arizona. Stanley was there long enough to get a couple of rounds of golf in but by noon on Friday, he had left me and one of my newer colleagues to take care of everything through the end of the conference on Saturday. Not a big deal because by this point him leaving to make sure he was home to enjoy his weekend was par for the course. The new hire and I got along just fine and were working well together in the conference environment so I figured we might even have a little fun. Shortly after lunch, my phone blows up with a call, then a text message, then another call and an adamant sounding voicemail from Hayden. I needed to call her. And I clearly needed to call her now from the sounds of it.

By this time, I was about three months into receiving regular, negative-toned communications from Hayden, so I honestly didn't think twice about calling her back. I mean, more likely than not, in about five minutes I was going to be listening to something that was not only not a big deal but was making me silently giggle and shake my head on my end of the phone. Boy was I wrong.

Within seconds of her answering the phone, I knew by her angry, authoritative tone that she was in real-time pissed off at me about something and whatever it was, it was big. And she definitely felt justified.

The bullet-pointed version of the next 30 or so minutes went like this:

What's wrong?

I just spoke to Mimi as she was leaving for vacation, and she is on fire about your email and quite frankly so am I.

What email?

The email you sent to the little exclusive group you formed. The one I wasn't allowed to participate in?

Which email?

You know, the one with the highly inappropriate content or whatever you call it from that singer? There is no way you don't know what I'm talking about.

The poem? I sent that like a month ago. How is there a problem now?

I am shocked/disappointed/mortified/furious/ disgusted/pissed off at your error in judgement/lack of professionalism/arrogant behavior/lack of awareness and Mimi wants you reported to senior leadership, HR and legal and I agree with her. And, furthermore, I also feel that you excluded me by not including me on the distribution list for that email.

Wait…whaaaaaaat…

Just breathe. Do not get in the van.

As I stood on this hotel patio, sun shining on my face, wondering if I was getting screamed at because I sent the email and Hayden and Mimi found it offensive, or because Hayden was upset that I didn't send it to her in the first place, I realized that Hayden was talking about a lot more than the email and I better pay attention. She was alleging negative comments from sales reps about me. Something came up about me throwing her under the bus. Another comment about me talking down to her or someone or maybe everyone at that point.

In that moment, I was pretty dumbstruck because it felt and sounded insane. Beyond the fact that we were a month out from this apparently horribly inappropriate poem, the unsolicited, personal details that both Hayden and Mimi had chosen to share with me over the years would have made that singer's poem blush. I knew so much about the intimacy of their personal lives that it was as though I lived in their houses. This didn't make sense.

I profusely and sincerely apologized for as much as I could for the unintended consequences of my email and for sending a personal email on my corporate account in the first place. The stress she had to endure dealing with Mimi and now me. The way she felt. The way Mimi felt. Shit, I started apologizing to myself for getting me into this situation. None of us were having any fun.

In the end, I only asked Hayden for one thing: Since Mimi would be back Monday, before you report me for anything, can you wait until I speak to Mimi? If you still want to submit to HR/Legal, I support whatever you think is best. Just let me understand things from Mimi's perspective first.

She said OK. Of course she did.

After I spoke with Mimi on Monday. After we had opened up communications, listened, learned, and came to a mutual understanding. After Mimi said, "You know how I am: I blow up and then after a couple of days I'm over it." After Mimi sent Hayden an email with a cc to me stating that we were in a good place and nothing more needed to be done.

Only then was when I learned that "OK" didn't mean the same thing to Hayden as it did to me.

Somehow a simple email meant to engage a small group of people had exacerbated into a shitstorm where I was going to have to talk to my senior leaders, HR and legal to what? Keep my job? This was crazy. She was acting like this was a federal case or something. She was acting like I deliberately harmed someone. She was acting like…this was a pearl-clutching moment. Remember that missing piece to the end game from earlier…me? Yeah, Hayden definitely knew her end game this time and I didn't have to ask her what it was.

Oddly enough, I didn't hear anything from anyone for a few days. I didn't know what to expect, really, but I figured I'd hear something. Then at the end of the week one of my colleague/friends called and asked me what I had done now. I started to laugh and said I would tell him but, first, what was he talking about? It went like this:

My friend laughed back and said, "The text message I just received about you."

I had no idea what he was talking about as I replied, "What text?"

Without skipping a beat, he said calmly into the phone, "The one from Evan asking me if I really didn't have any negative information to submit about you."

I could feel my breath catching in my throat as I uttered, "What? Are you fucking with me? That's silly." He kind of laughed again and said, "Nope. I can send you a screenshot."

I sat there waiting for a few seconds and then the text came through. The only words I could make were, "Ok…Fuck. What the hell?"

My friend in a jokingly exacerbated tone replied, "*That's* why I'm calling…what did you do?"

I told him simply, "Sent an email. How did you respond?"

"Anslie for Chief Executive. Look closer at the screenshot," he said with a smile in his voice.

I ultimately learned of a few other people who were contacted in a similar manner, including one recently, who over a year later, finally shared that she received multiple phone calls and texts about me during that time that made her uncomfortable. They came from Hayden, Evan, and even Stanley, himself. Sometimes multiple messages between them went to a single person to try to get new and different feedback. A copy of Mimi's original scathing email about me also managed to somehow get out. But while there were a lot of narratives going around and plenty of shenanigans, still nothing had happened to me…not even an Outlook request after more than a week.

It was right about then that an HR Manager and Stanley let me know that they would like to speak with me the next day.

Find strength in your breath. Just breathe.

I reached out to an attorney friend for advice, who referred me to an employment attorney friend of his. On one hand connecting with that employment attorney taught me how to research consent laws by state and record conversations and the importance of doing both. On the other hand, unbeknownst to me or my attorney friend, that employment attorney represented and knew a lot of the business leaders in my industry, including the key opinion leader whose company performed the alleged unethical, kickback practices with Evan and Hayden. Suffice to say he's not who ultimately came to represent me.

Immediately prior to the call with HR and Stanley, I received a multi-page Disciplinary Plan, stating everything from that I had violated the sexual harassment corporate code of conduct to that they had testaments from people going months back about my poor behavior to I had broken inducement of customer policies. I had to "cease and desist" the inclusive leadership group and apologize for the words that angered Mimi and Hayden, using a predetermined verbatim, to all involved external customers. I had to apologize individually to every internal person listed on the corrective action. Some of those folks were to receive apologies for me sending them the email. Some were to receive apologies for me sending the email but excluding them. I had to read a business book that I had read multiple times before and do scheduled updates with Stanley on my learnings from it. Oh, and if I didn't complete all of the tasks itemized and address the accusations detailed in this document to Stanley's satisfaction, I could be fired. Spectacular.

I dialed into the conference line. And since the state I was in, the state Stanley was in and the state where our company was located were all single consent states, I hit record.

It's funny reflecting on that call now. It was essentially the grand opening of my crisis. I mean, sure, we had some minor events and a few attention-grabbing circus performers over the last few months…let's call it my crisis' soft opening…but nothing like what was unleashed on this call. The HR Manager, Rachel, went through a litany of details and occurrences: the corporate code of conduct, how she felt the poem violated it, the feedback she got from "all of the people she interviewed" not just on their feelings about the poem but on me, "other" things she heard about my personality that weren't worth detailing but I guess was worth mentioning that they existed, and what I needed to do to attempt to rectify the situation. A couple of things you should know here: first, for that first 30 minutes of words I didn't speak other than saying yes or no and, second, neither did Stanley. It was all Rachel. At the end of Rachel's portion, she asked me if I had any questions. I said I didn't but would like to reserve the right to ask any later. Then she said she was going to hand over the call to Stanley for his portion of this corrective action.

His portion of the corrective action? What does that even mean? An HR issue is an HR issue…there's not a Stanley-based subsection in the code of conduct.

Inhale. Exhale. Just breathe.

Now another thing you need to know here is what is common knowledge to those of us who know Stanley and/or work for him. At any given time Stanley is a combination of passive aggressiveness, ADHD, knee-jerk reactions, insecurity and communication through redundancy…all while touting his commitment to faith and family (yep, he includes that in presentations). Get the picture?

If you know these things about Stanley, or anyone like Stanley, going into a situation *and* you can self-discipline your own behavior, much to their dismay, you can normally navigate the waters fairly well. Because here's what you have to remember: all of those characteristics…passive aggressiveness, ADHD, knee-jerk reactions, insecurity, repeating oneself over and over again…are all exacerbated in similar fashions. Either their audience gives some non-emotional response that doesn't mirror their emotions and derails them, or their audience does not respond at all and derails them. They need a reaction because that's the only way they feel heard and validated. They need a reaction in that moment like you need air to survive.

The key is your self-discipline to not react. Your conscious choice to not get thrown into the van. You have to let the personal attacks and the shitty remarks and the professional accusations and the lies that are coming just roll right over you. You can ruminate and spit fire and brimstone about them later, but not while they are happening. Do not give energy to whoever is coming after you. That is your energy. That is how you reach your end game. Now breathe.

Since Stanley had had 30 minutes to wind himself up while Rachel was leading her portion, he started vomit cometing at a force so fast and so strong that I would have had to interrupt him to actually say something. So, for 8 minutes I just sat there. Not saying a word.

I listened as he went line by line through a spread sheet he created, filled with alleged text messages and secret phone conversations that were had about me months, in some cases more than a year, prior. Several instances labeled "Does Not Work Well With Others," some of which did not require collaboration, others that simply never happened. He provided names and dates and feelings and opinions. If this experience wasn't happening to me it would have been fascinating. It was a lot of work. Stanley definitely put in the sweat equity.

And then suddenly, in the middle of a sentence (welcome, ADHD, to the party!) he realized that he was the only one talking. There had been no feedback, no reaction, no shock, no emotional outbursts other than his. Then it went like this:

Stanley pivoted what he saying to, "Anslie, are you even there? Are you listening to me?"

"Yes," I replied.

Stanley's tone went up an octave to rattle off, "Well, you aren't saying anything. How am I supposed to know you're there?"

Calmly I asked, "Did you ask me a question?"

He paused and uttered, "Well, no."

"That's why I haven't said anything," I replied.

Stanley was undeterred on his reapproach, "Don't you have anything to say about what I've presented so far?"

"No. I'll wait til you're done," I told him, wondering the entire time how stupid he thought I was.

In retrospect it was fortunate at that time that we weren't all living so out of real touch as we've become used to in the pandemic and that we were still doing mostly conference calls as opposed to predominately ZOOM meetings. Because in this, the grand opening of my crisis, I was sitting at my desk laughing my ass off. I felt like I could almost see Stanley's head about to spontaneously combust due to not shoving me kicking and screaming into the van.

Stanley continued on with more of the same. Admittedly, there were other times it was good no one could see me because I was fuming. Even though my anger was silent I have no doubt it was all over my face. Some of the things that were said were horrible to hear. I knew in my heart they were not true. I knew I had good people in my corner who believed in me. But hearing example after example of how detrimental my thoughts, my actions, my words...*me*...was to the world around me couldn't help but hurt. A lot.

But that wasn't the time to hurt. I could do that for the entire rest of the day after I hung up the phone if I wanted to but not now.

Self-discipline. Breathe. Think in this pause. He was done. It was my turn to talk.

Remember, they had sent me the Disciplinary Plan only minutes before the conference call. I am sure this was by design so that I would have zero time to process any of the accusations or mandatory actions in advance. In that moment...my moment to speak...the only questions I could think to ask were:

"Rachel, did HR participate in the obtaining of feedback information on me that Stanley shared (remember...I've seen some of the text messages)?" She quietly answered, "No."

My second on-the-fly question was, "Rachel, as I have never had an experience like this before, is it normal for there to be a separate, non-HR supervised, information seeking effort by a supervisor related to an employee? I would think HR would oversee every component of a disciplinary plan." She danced around to respond, "There's no real answer here. Sometimes HR does all of it, but a supervisor can always do their own investigation and share their findings with us."

Next I was on to Stanley with, "Stanley, some of these situations you mentioned happened several months ago. I've had 2 performance management reviews with you since some of them, and at least one review with you since most of them. If I've been such a problem and a non-collaborator with so many people, why are you only telling me now?" Without missing a beat he replied, "Well, we've talked about some of these things but others were just recently brought to my attention."

And in my final attempt to grasp some sanity in this circus I stated, "Stanley, I have to look over this more closely, but a few of these things just didn't happen. For instance, the portion stating that the feedback exchange I hosted with sales reps was negatively received, people felt threatened and I should have never done it? I have emails not only from the team about how positive they felt, but from you and Don commending me and sending my efforts out to management as a "best practice."" My oh my did he come prepared because without hesitation he simply said, "Things change and I didn't have the full picture then but now I have more information."

Remember those adjectives used to describe me at the beginning of the book? Yeah, he was in that "other" group of people.

But, really, mine were legitimate questions, right? Ones in which we should all have the right to ask when we are being formally accused of something: Is this the way an intervention normally goes? If what you're saying has been a systemic problem with me, why am I only hearing about it now? And why are occurrences included that didn't happen?

The call wrapped up with them telling me I would have to sign and date the disciplinary plan and return it to both of them ASAP. It would become part of my permanent record at the company. I explained that before I signed off on anything, I would like to read through it again as what was included was a lot to digest and I would likely have additional questions. They agreed. We hung up. And the reality of my situation began to sink in and for a minute, it took my breath away.

I decided to email another leader in HR, Doris, to hopefully schedule some time to get feedback and advice. Doris and I knew each other well enough. When I first joined the business unit she had had me be part of an anti-sexual harassment initiative at a national meeting to help others navigate, avoid and eliminate the issue. I was chosen because of how forthright and unwavering I was on the issue. Funny, huh?

Anyway, because of our history, I had reached out to her a few times in the previous few months to discuss my negative work environment but had never heard back from her. I was disappointed by the non-response, but not in any real twist about it. I just figured we would eventually talk. Sure enough this time she responded, and she had time in her schedule to talk to me the next day.

We spoke for an extended period of time. I figured my best bet was to give her the full picture of not just what had transpired over the last couple of months, but what I believed to be the catalyst: the unethical kickback situation. She listened. She asked questions. She said it sounded like nothing short of a witch hunt. I asked her if she wanted the notes that I had kept. She declined but did agree that she needed to loop in Compliance about the kickback situation. I let her know I was happy to help. She also stated I had to sign off on the disciplinary plan despite my feelings about the included accusations, but that I could add my counterstatements to the document and that amended document would be what would be placed in my permanent file. This way, she said, if I were up for a promotion in the future, the potential hiring manager could see the full story and I would be better equipped to answer any questions. Shit, I hadn't even considered that. Future hiring managers could access my performance management files. Of course they could and would. Fuck me.

I eventually added my counter notes and password protected the document in hopes of making it at least difficult to alter. When I sent it, I can remember just staring at my computer screen, wondering how I got to this place and reminding myself again to breathe.

I had survived the first couple rounds of attacks, triggered by Hayden and commandeered by Stanley. I knew more were coming but I was ok in that moment. Eighteen months later I have had more than my fair share of "God, why didn't I say that?" or "If only I would've thought to do this" moments about those calls but overall I feel ok about them. Please do not take my "ok" as a negative, I'm just being as realistic with myself as one can be in her own biased self-judgement. Ok is good. I am convinced that "Ok" happened then, and in so many subsequent chapters of this crisis, in large part because of what I questioned and ultimately learned about the strength of my breath. It helped keep my thoughts focused and my voice steady. It helped me find time when there seemingly was none to think before I reacted. It helped keep my heart from pounding loudly in my ears and beating out of my chest. Let's be blunt: it kept me out of the van.

I wish I could tell you that it has been all rainbows and unicorns the more I have learned to control and use my breath through stressful and painful situations. I wish I could, but I would be lying. We are a labeling society, especially in business for women. And as many of you know, male or female, the less emotional and erratic and aggressive a woman acts, the more she is likely to become known as cold and unfriendly and difficult-to-work-with…maybe even one of my personal favorites: selfish…she only cares about herself. Very rarely can women simply be described as being solid or successful at whatever it is they do. There always seems to be an added, unnecessary adjective or two mandatorily included. The dog whistle "Yeah, but" that a lot of other people don't hear. But I do. And you do or will. And we will all be fine.

Because we will follow our breath through those times, too.

We will let our breath guide our movements and focus our thoughts.

We will remember to find our strength and just breathe.

Chapter 3
Selfish Times

I say "selfish," you hear…what? Come on. I say "selfish," and you hear…oh, let me list some options for us to start with: bitch, egotistical, narcissist, greedy, myopic, doesn't share credit, their way or the highway. Let's run through a few more for any of our dog whistle lovers who are reading: too ambitious, too assertive, not a team player, opportunistic, prescriptive. I've heard them all and probably at one point or another been either directly or indirectly referred to as all of them in my career. They are labels that others give others, warranted or not. Remember…we are a labeling society: it's what we do.

I struggled with being thought of as selfish or labeled as selfish or God forbid even being selfish for many, many years. Maybe it was that Italian Catholic upbringing that burnt guilt in my brain for everything and anything that had to do with putting myself first. Maybe it was seeing my mother work and then pickup kids from practices and then cook dinner and then help with homework before my father even got home from work every day. Maybe it was being fortunate after a middle-class upbringing to figure out a way to go to a fancy, private liberal arts school with scholarships, grants, loans, parents and working full-time. I don't know. But it was there. The stigma of ever being considered selfish. Not for me.

But, over the last few months of ruminating and gardening and crafting and chilling out with my crisis I have come to understand that my views on the matter have changed. I am selfish sometimes. I am selfish at times that are wholly inconvenient for others. And that's ok. Actually, that's more than ok…it's a liberating, life-changing realization. Who do I have to thank for this moment of clarity?

My crisis and some of its cast members, of course.

Prior to the last couple of years, and if I'm being honest, probably up until about a little over a year ago, I had zero work-personal balance. Not because my company was forcing that lifestyle on me, but rather because I insisted on it myself. Don't get me wrong, I took legitimate vacations here and there, and the occasional long weekend, but like a lot of businesspeople I never completely unplugged, turned off, checked out. I couldn't. I had clients who had customers and customers who had families that in my head were counting on me all the time. I was part of a business unit that generally struggled to have meaningful connections with industry leaders who I could text and meet with on a whim…I had to be available. I had unique projects in different phases of completion that could change for the better everything from daily critical services to quarterly outcomes to both customer and employee retention…I needed to be there.

What I really needed was to get the hell over myself.

When I told Doris, the HR leader I debriefed with post the grand opening of my crisis, about the unethical kickback issue I discovered and my overall situation, she was notably affected. I could hear it in her voice when she talked about looping in Compliance and Legal. I sensed it by the simple fact she didn't talk about talking to people about whether or not to act, but rather she wanted to act and act now. I remember feeling hopeful. I remember thinking, "Finally." Not only was a new, objective set of eyes going to be placed on how I was being treated but someone was acknowledging the real risk these unethical behaviors posed to our company and she was going to investigate. She got how not only our reputation could be tarnished in this business sector, but if the situation became public or worse became some underground new way of doing business, the optics alone could irreparably damage our company as a whole.

Then she told me to sit tight. It was the mid-December, and she was sure most of the people she would need to talk to were either on vacation through the rest of the year or about to be on vacation. Probably was going to take until after the New Year to really get anything together but I shouldn't worry. They'll get things figured out.

I'm sorry…what?

Beyond the personal detriment I just shared that I had been going through for the last 3 months and what happened to me the day prior, I just told you that in at least one account, it appears as though employees not only condoned unethical behaviors like inducements and personal kickbacks in the form of significant increases in orders, but they deliberately set up the system themselves. They then tried to implement the same system in one of my accounts, leading anyone to believe that there are likely others already out there because humans tend to go with what they know, especially if it's profitable. And, let me get this straight, you're worried about interrupting someone's holiday PTO?

So, I waited. And while I waited, I, too, had scheduled time off, but now I had things to do. In addition to my inability to comprehend my world of work living without me, I now had disciplinary plan duties to complete. So while I continued to work on my projects, I also had to call people and email people to apologize for my ostracizing behaviors. I had to document when we spoke and if they accepted my apology and eventually provide Rachel and Stanley with a detailed list of these interactions that they wanted completed by the end of December. Well, guess what? A lot of those people I needed to reach were on holiday PTO and they cared even less about my mandated timeline to talk to them than Doris cared to interrupt Legal and Compliance employees' PTO to avoid a public corporate nightmare.

I would be remiss if I failed to mention that during that same time, Stanley was also taking PTO. But his was a fickle PTO as he was on it but doing work selectively. In other words, he *was not* on PTO the multiple times he sent follow-up inquiries to my disciplinary plan or scrutinizing questions about my projects, but he *was* on PTO if I needed any assistance or had a question. Whether or not I was on

PTO was irrelevant…especially if he was inquiring about the disciplinary plan activities.

I remember thinking how unbelievably selfish, among other things, that these people were. Here I was working my ass off not only during the holidays and trying to protect the company from an avoidable catastrophe in the works, but also doing so during an all-out assault on my psyche and reputation. Who did these people think they were taking downtime and having personal joys with family and friends when I couldn't? Didn't they get the urgency of this situation we were in? That I was in?

The simple answer was: No. None of it was particularly that urgent to them. It was urgent to me. And how I felt didn't make the radar of them changing whatever it was they wanted to do… whatever they felt to be urgent to them…including taking PTO.

How selfish.

How brilliant.

Situation presents itself to a person. They let it process through their values and priorities and feelings. Is it urgent to me? Nope. But it's urgent to this other person? Doesn't matter.

That's essentially what happened during those winter holidays. Sure enough, everyone ended up reconnecting shortly after the first of the year to talk, and we'll get to the consequences of those interactions later. But during that holiday season when I was staring at my phone and my email like a desperate teenager willing their boyfriend or girlfriend to call? They were selfishly enjoying their PTOs and families and friends and sleeping in.

As they should.

See, my then infant crisis and shady business practice discovery were still there when the calendar switched to 2019. Neither of them were any worse or any better. No new earth-shattering data had been discovered and no deadlines had been missed, or if they had, had no lasting effects on me or anyone else that I could see. The world was as it was before. Except for me. I was different.

I had been a ball of tightly wound stress through the entire holidays. I was filled with worry and angst made seemingly worse every day because of the questions that robbed my sleep every night: Why can't I reach these people? Is that project proposal worded appropriately? Why isn't Doris doing more? Does Legal even know yet, and what if they don't? Can I be doing more? Should I try to reach out again to show just how important this is?

I couldn't turn anything off. I couldn't unplug. I couldn't let go of the death grasp I had on everything. I couldn't be selfish, and it cost me.

When everyone returned from holiday break they were refocused and ready. The people who I thought were going to help me, as well as those who I knew were trying to hurt me, all came back bright-eyed and bushy tailed. They had taken the time they earned throughout the previous year and enjoyed it. They had recharged. But I hadn't. I was drawing from every internal pocket of strength and professionalism perseverance I could find. I felt I was at a mental and emotional deficit that while I had not caused, I certainly hadn't needed to feed. I do believe that while my crisis has had what feels like countless gut-wrenching moments over the last two years, those first six weeks of 2019 were by far the most damaging because it was then that this cast of bad actors first truly tried to break me, and I wasn't even close to being prepared for it because I hadn't yet learned how to be selfish.

The accusations and demands compounded daily through emails and phone calls and text messages. People were cc'd and bcc'd and forwarded messages that they should not have even known existed. Sales reps were being encouraged to speak up by Hayden, which I only learned later meant her pointedly asking them after we'd worked together what I did wrong and if I made them feel offended in any way. Stanley began taking away resources and responsibilities from me, claiming that I wasn't needed anymore, while also disallowing me to help onboard new hires to our immediate team, a role that I had always been afforded and embraced. He also publicly shared with two internal candidates that were passed up for promotions, who I knew well and had helped coach in many ways, that if they wanted to succeed, they should abide by the following:

Definitely do not emulate Anslie. The only reason she can do what she does is because she lives alone and has no real responsibilities. If she did, she wouldn't be as good. She doesn't have a life.

The blows were constant and the toll they took on me was immense, made even worse because I was a shell of myself emotionally, physically, and mentally. I maintained my composure through all of it—never breaking down or yelling in meetings, never retaliating, always breathing through. But it was a fragile state. I had become a fragile state.

It was around the end of January, when I received the notice that 28 employees, pre-selected by Stanley, were going to be completing the formal internal, HR-led feedback detailed in my disciplinary plan, that I finally embraced being selfish. I finally let go of the non-negotiable, negative connotations of being selfish that had been burnt into my brain and replaced them with *my* version of being selfish:

Taking care of my mental well-being, my health, my emotions first so that I could continue to help others, love others, succeed and live a life fulfilled.

Looking back at that moment, I can't decide if it was so pivotal because I was really that close to breaking and desperately needed something to hold onto, or because seeing that 28 people, some who barely knew me and had never worked with me, were going to be passing judgement on me, essentially impacting a situation they had nothing to do with nor even knew existed, and I realized that I needed to find a way to not just survive, but to get in this fight. Alone with my thoughts, I believe it was both.

Just as I mentioned earlier that the mind has a funny way of helping you rationalize not doing something you didn't want to do in the first place, it can also help you do something that you never knew you needed to do to thrive. In January 2019, my mind stepped up to the plate and helped me make some permanent changes…some selfish changes.

I turned my email notification on my phone off, realizing that I looked at my phone 50 times a day…I didn't need an extra 50 dings a day to help me look at any email 6 minutes sooner. I stopped automatically working on the weekends. If the deadline was Monday morning and I hadn't completed the project by Friday, weekend work would be no problem. But if what wasn't finished Friday wasn't due Monday, I could wait until Monday to pick it up again. And there were no client projects or matters that were so urgent as to leave a weekend message for, let alone any one urgent enough to answer such weekend messages so I stopped those behaviors, too. And weekend conferences, any Sunday departures or late Friday night arrivals home? Yeah, those became part of my new is-this-critical algorithm and most of them didn't make the cut.

On a personal note, I started making plans for weeknights again and removed the "I'll have to see if I'm traveling" phrase for any event that was two weeks or more out. I began traveling with a good book to read on my many flights instead of making sure that my laptop was always fully charged. I reached out to friends I hadn't talked to in ages because I was always too tired or too busy or just not around. I had always managed to take vacations, solo or with a companion, but I never came close to using the amount of vacation time provided me. I started to put a dent in that pile of hours with long-weekend puppy hiking trips and extended stays on my own dime when business took me somewhere fun or new.

The most interesting fact about all of these and the many other changes I made? They didn't negatively impact anything that I had been so worried would suffer but they did positively impact me in nearly every component of my life. The stress of my crisis still didn't have me eating or sleeping like I needed to be but both improved. And I had more energy to deal with my crisis now rather than just survive its next hit. Neither my clients' satisfaction nor my overall job performance decreased. In fact, I became ranked higher and brought in more revenue than ever. I laughed more and saw people I cared about, and who cared about me, more. My life, both my professional life and my personal life, had become more by me giving less. By me giving less, I actually had more to give. Weird. The key component was I began to give less to the optional, soul-sucking activities that came my way and gave more to the fulfilling, set-my-soul-on-fire activities that came my way or that I now had the energy to seek out.

My crisis was still there…we still had a long way to go together. But I had reclaimed a part of myself to go the distance, to get back in and stay in the fight. I had become my version of selfish.

The funny thing that now often makes me quietly laugh to myself is that I am unsure if or when I would have ever changed my view of selfishness, or became able to accept being selfish, if not for the very people who were trying to destroy my world through their versions of selfishness. I will have to find a way to thank them someday.

Chapter 4
In the Fight

"**N**othing is going to change. Why are you doing this?"

I would like to tell you those words take me back to this one challenging but life-affirming moment, where I was at a fork in the road with my crisis and had to choose: cave in or keep going. Or that it was just that one jaded friend who could never muster up support for me to do anything more than binge watch whatever new controversial docuseries was streaming on Netflix. Or that it was my parents, set in their ways of what you do and don't do, including not causing waves at work because you'd be labeled as some bad adjective or maybe even be risking your job by speaking up.

But none of those were *the* case…*all* of them were the case and they had good company. Girlfriends, guy friends, colleagues, family, my attorney, other attorney friends, mentors, mediators, even corporate compliance officers…you name the person, and I can likely give you an example that combines that person supporting me and simultaneously telling me that I was crazy or that the situation was futile. After more than a year, I was hearing a lot of both.

But I was in it. I chose to be in it. By the time all of the retaliating and harassing behaviors started for me in the Fall of 2018, I already had dozens of pages of notes taken on the profound misogyny that I had experienced and witnessed over the previous couple of years, the perpetual gaslighting and the ethically questionable business behaviors that seemed to be everywhere. I had talked to people about it. I had stood up at meetings. I became known as someone who would stand up and speak up. But short of a target getting ever more pronounced on my back, nothing really changed.

Or so I thought.

What I failed to consider during those early times of standing up and speaking up *a little* was that a lot of people were watching. A lot of different people.

Of course I heard from my friends and colleagues who either knew my story or had witnessed the latest WTF-was-that-that-just-happened moment. And I certainly heard from the naysayers and the would-be kidnappers, the corporate protectors and family that would go from being supportive to being worried what this crisis would mean for *us as a family*. But there were a lot more people watching from the shadows and the backs of meeting rooms, listening silently on conference calls. Waiting. Wondering. And hoping.

In mid-January 2019, about a week or so before I had my selfish epiphany, I was working with clients out-of-state for a couple of days. Scheduled at the end of one day was a call with Rachel. I had some follow-up questions for her. New accusations that seemingly came from nowhere, Stanley had documented and added to the original 40-point disciplinary plan. Recent calls with Compliance about the kickback claims had some ambiguous parts when it came to my involvement moving forward. It was a lot to cover in the hour she allotted me, but I was committed to giving it a shot. So, I sat in the dark strip mall parking lot with my notes and my recorder because at this point I had become genuinely concerned about talking anywhere that someone could overhear me.

So we talked…and talked.

Two very critical points came out of that discussion: first, when I asked Rachel if my situation would have been different if her colleague Doris had ever returned my requests to connect in the Fall, she told me, "Yes, because then you would have been reporting something to the company rather than accusing people of retaliation." And second, as we were wrapping up, she told me how committed she was to ensuring a safe, healthy environment for me that fostered my success. I directly responded, "In case I haven't been clear tonight or when we talked 2 days ago, I am in a hostile and retaliatory environment. I am not sleeping or eating. I have had to talk to an attorney because you are not protecting me. If you were me, what would you do? Sue the company? Quit? Keep not sleeping or eating? What should I do?" She didn't have a response. But then again, two days prior Rachel and Doris had basically told me in response to my proof of Stanley's fabrication of the disciplinary plan content I shouldn't worry about the lies and just keep my head down and get through it. So, really, what profoundly helpful, supportive statement did I think Rachel was going to make two days later?

This night, one month after the initial disciplinary plan conference call and many months before I would get myself fully out of the pit of despair, I felt myself internally collapse. In those immediate moments after hanging up from that call with Rachel, the "you're crazies" and "this is futiles" started creeping around my mind looking for a little spot to call home. I had HR telling me they knew the charges against me were false, but they weren't going to do anything about it. No one knew yet if the kickback charges would be proven but what they did know was that it mattered more when corporate was alerted by me about the charges versus if they really happened or not. And the cast members in my crisis were just hitting their stride after long, relaxing holiday breaks whereas I was living off of airport convenience store beef jerky and veggie trays and a few hours of sleep in the hotel *du jour*. It was a bleak moment, sitting in the dark looking out my rental car window.

I don't know how long I sat there but it was one of those "felt like a minute/felt like hours" moments all at the same time. I couldn't focus. I remember not even being able to cry which seemed strange for how desolate I felt. I just stared at the strip mall stores and the people running in and out. I wondered if any of them heard what was happening, what would they think? Would they think I was crazy, or would they see what I was holding onto: it's always the right time to do right. I realized it really didn't matter.

I knew I should probably try to eat. I wanted to just find my hotel and fall into bed and forget this moment entirely. I almost did just that as I pulled into the hotel parking lot, but then my phone rang.

I may have been losing the fight in that moment, but I definitely wasn't out of the fight. Not by a long shot. Not when one of the people who had been silently watching me for months called that night. Not when she shared her story and how what I was doing was so important to her…and the future of her baby girl that was cooing in her arms as we talked.

You're god damn right I was still in this fight.

When the inquiries into my character started near the end of 2018, multiple people were interviewed by Rachel, including Theresa who was now on the phone with me. Theresa was this incredibly talented, confident, funny younger professional. She's one of those women that women like me who are a decade or more her senior are thrilled to meet and feel even more privileged to get to know. She's one of those rare people these days who eagerly seeks out mentors and knowledge, but where the mentors also learn immense lessons from her as well if they keep their minds and ears open.

She had recently shared with me that she told Rachel how insane she found the efforts against me to be, in large part because she had reported a previous legitimate complaint, when a senior leader physically assaulted and sexually harassed her, and not so much as a hint of anything corrective ever happened to him. As a side note, that senior leader was none other than Jack the "try to be a little less *you*" cast member from my first management meeting now 2.5 years prior.

Theresa and I began to talk. She apologized for calling so late in my evening. I explained to her that she could call me any time and that I felt her call that evening was divine intervention from the universe because of the call I had just had with Rachel. I shared with her how I was feeling, the mind-blowing disbelief and at times debilitating pain that seemed constant, fending off attacks and dealing with the deliberate disengagement of the very people who were hired to help employees in situations like mine. That's when she told me I couldn't give up. That's when she told me that her mother had told her recently that she should step back and maybe not cause as much disruption. That's when she told me what had recently happened to her, and some of the women on her team. That's when we made a pact that her daughter wasn't ever going to have to go through what we were dealing with…not if we had anything to do about it.

Right around the time of my initial disciplinary plan call with Rachel and Stanley in December, Theresa's team had a holiday dinner. Besides her team, some senior leaders also attended, including Don who was the GM of the business unit by that time. At what sounded like a long banquet-style table that sat 15 or so people, Don, who was Theresa's boss's boss, chose to sit next to Theresa. Per Theresa, dinner progressed as these sorts of dinners often do: people chatting about holiday plans and current projects and laughing about this or that from the year. And then, without warning or any sort of discussion as a precursor, Don turned to Theresa at the table and stated, "So, I hear that you're a lot more liberal than I ever thought you were." I'm sorry, what?

Theresa was admittedly caught off guard, both because of the statement itself and because it was made in a public setting with her peers in earshot.

When she asked what Don was referring to, he launched into what I can only describe as a personal attack masked as interest and seeking to understand. After never having had a conversation with Theresa about her personal beliefs on anything, Don brought up her feelings on everything from a woman's right to choose to her political beliefs to her support of the #MeToo movement, even stating after her disagreeing that enough hadn't been done yet to help women, that "enough was enough." He even added something about it's getting really hard for men, they're afraid to do anything, and they can't even talk to women anymore. Unphased, Theresa's retort included a statement about how Jack had physically assaulted her and how would Don feel if something like that happened to his daughter at work…wouldn't he want to see things improve or change for her? His response? His daughter was smart enough not to get herself into a situation like that in the first place. I was speechless.

As I listened to Theresa, now sitting in my second dark parking lot of the night in front of my hotel, the tears finally came, silently streaming down my face as I listened to her. And just when I couldn't imagine how Don could possibly be more misogynistically antagonistic towards her, the end of their conversation went something like this:

Don looked over at Theresa and said, "What do you think makes you most strong as a woman?"

Caught off guard by the continued weird dinner conversation, Theresa gathered herself and replied, "Being successful at my career, being innovative/making a difference, being a good person."

Doubling down on whatever it was he was thinking, Don answered, "No. Those things don't make you strong as a woman."

"Well, I think they do," Theresa replied, even more confused than 1 minute prior.

Don was undeterred when he quipped, "They don't. Do you know the single thing that makes you strong?"

Theresa truly had no idea what the hell was going on at this point so she simply said, "No."

And then he laid it out for her and women everywhere stopped: "Being a mother. That was the day you became strong."

I have to give Theresa credit because I'm fairly certain I couldn't have come up with something as profound as she did: "I love my daughter and I love being a mother but I 100% disagree with you. I am teaching my daughter how to be a strong woman because I am successful, innovative and I work hard while being a mother."

Remaining relentlessly undeterred, Don looked at her with a table full of her peers in earshot and said, "No. You're wrong."

Even writing this now 18 months later, tears come to my eyes because what you may not be thinking about but what is really at the root of this entire disgusting encounter is: how did Don even know anything personal about Theresa to make those shocking statements and ask those insulting questions in the first place?

As Theresa explained to me, every point of contention that Don broached with her were topics that she discussed with Rachel when she was "interviewed" about my character, or lack thereof. Rachel was a real-life corporate 007 with limitless duplicity. I was stunned.

At this point I wasn't gut punched…I was hollowed out and gutted. Not only had Rachel an hour prior left me hanging out on a very weak limb alone, but now I learned that she betrayed one of the women who stood up for me, sharing her private conversation with someone for no other reason than to break her down? I could not stop apologizing to Theresa for being the cause of what had happened to her, both the encounter with HR and the verbal assault with Don at dinner. I was being attacked but this was my choice. Theresa was being attacked by no fault of her own but rather for my choice.

That's when Theresa told me to not only stop apologizing but also that she *was* making a choice to fight. Yes, she was standing up for me and for her and for the other women in our company, but then she said these words that I will remember for the rest of my life:

"As I look at my daughter now in my arms, how can I ever look her in the eye 20 years from now when she comes home and tells me she was harassed or discriminated against, asking me for advice or help, and know that I had an opportunity to fight to have made things better for her now and I chose not to do it? I am doing this for her as much as for us. You are helping both me and my daughter with what you are doing."

Those were fightin' words if I'd ever heard any.

But Theresa wasn't done yet. She hadn't yet shared with me the trigger for her call that night in the first place. All I could think of was, "There's more?"

Remember Jack, Mr. Need-To-Be-Eased-Into and Theresa's assaulter? Well, about a year or so before this night he had decided to take a higher-paying position with another company in our industry. They weren't a competitor so there wasn't a non-compete violation. He wasn't shy about sharing with others that he had left for financial reasons, either.

Shortly after Theresa was interviewed by Rachel about me, Theresa discovered that Jack was being rehired as a consultant at our company, in spite of the documentation of what he had done to her, and as we learned, others. She felt extremely uncomfortable at the idea of having to see him again, let alone that her company would employ him again. I mean, fine...don't fire the guy and let him leave on his own but for fuck's sake, be a little smart...don't rehire the problem once it has rectified itself. Christ.

Since I was in the thick of multiple weekly calls with Compliance and HR at the time, I had previously told Theresa to let me handle it to keep her out of the drama as much as possible. When I told both HR and Compliance about Jack's rehiring, they were equally shocked, with Compliance stating on a live phone call that Jack was labeled (remember how we love our labels?) as "non-rehireable" so he couldn't be employed. They committed to looking into it and within the same day I was forwarded an email from corporate leadership confirming the hire and that they felt it was ok since he would never be employee-facing with anyone. I politely reminded HR and Compliance of a situation of mine from 4 years ago where the company contracted a known sexual harasser (more on that later) and the chaos that ensued. Furthermore, was that the type of company we were? One that rehires men who have not just been alleged, but documented to have gotten drunk and sexually assaulted our female employees, among other accusations? This cannot possibly be ok.

Jack's consulting contract was promptly terminated. I felt like we had a win, however minor. Most importantly, the termination had eliminated any women at our company unknowingly walking into a meeting room where he was located and experiencing that sick feeling of their stomach dropping.

I truly believed at least that issue was resolved.

Fast forward to my current conversation with Theresa on the phone. The situation was not resolved. Jack was not working with our company but he was still very much impacting the women there. Earlier that day Don had called a meeting with Theresa's team in his office. Her team was comprised of 3 women and 1 man. Per Theresa, the meeting felt like an attack on their work and abilities, with a particular focus on the women's performance. She said they were criticized about work that was completed as well as work that was ongoing. Accusations about lack of planning projects and tracking measures of success within the salesforce were posed. The most troubling fact of the encounter was that there was no forewarning. Their efforts had previously been commended as being some of the most innovative and nimble in the company.

The meeting ended in Don's office. Theresa's team, confused at what had transpired, began to return to their cubicles to get back to work. As they did, Don asked Theresa to stay back in his office. When she did, he half-shut the door behind her and Theresa told me it went something like this:

Don walked behind his desk, looked up and said, "So, since you are responsible for taking away how we were going to succeed/be profitable in the second half of the year, what's your plan to [make up for it]?"

Theresa was again caught off guard as she had been at that dinner a minute ago and replied, "I'm sorry. What are you talking about?"

Don not missing a beat launched, "Jack. It's because of you we are not going to get to benefit from his consulting expertise so how are you going to fix it?"

Theresa, appalled, came back with, "Don, I don't know what you're talking about. Jack [harassed] women, including me. He shouldn't be working here in the first place."

"Well, I hope you can come up with something to make up for him not being here because now we're at a deficit." Don was clearly…again…undeterred.

Theresa said she then went back to her desk area and talked with the other two women on her team. She told them what had just happened to her. They were stunned at what transpired with Don in their meeting but his attack on Theresa, blaming her for the business unit not benefitting from the talents of a known sexual harasser? That was simply unbelievable.

As they discussed how they were feeling, somebody made an interesting observation that Theresa shared with me: if they were feeling this disempowered and berated after one meeting, how was I feeling after months of attacks from multiple people? How was I not only attending meetings but actively participating in them with success? All of them knew at least in part what I was going through at the time, but this was their first harsh pill of it to swallow. Prior to that day, they had all been subjected to the new and improved dog whistle misogyny, but not the out and out verbal assaults. This was different and now they knew. And, more importantly, they wanted to let me know that I had their support.

I was speechless and heartbroken and inspired and enraged all at the same time, convinced that rather than brainstorming on how to run a profitable company and inspire a sales team, these bad actors were spending their time conspiring on how to berate amazing women and blame amazing women for their own ethical and professional shortcomings. I told Theresa that enough was enough. I had had no idea what she or her colleagues had been going through and now that I did, we had to commit to communicating with each other no matter how hectic life and travel would get. These situations…*our* situations…were the kind that were meant to create isolation and self-doubt in someone, disabling them from talking to others about what was happening because of the ultimate internal blame they put on themselves. These were targeted exercises, and we were at least two of the many targets. If I didn't know about her and the women on their team, who else was out there quietly in the shadows, coping alone, that I didn't know about? I would be damned if I was going to let anyone mentally, emotionally or physically deal with this bullshit misogyny turned retaliatory behavior alone.

I had not gotten to recharge my batteries over the holidays like many others involved in this crisis. And I certainly had not had any additional sleep or food since sitting in not one but two dark parking lots that night, feeling despondent and alone. But I had something else now: I was pissed off.

Over the previous few months, I had certainly become angry, furious even a couple of times, but those moments were fleeting and never outwardly expressed. Ever. I was mostly bouncing between surviving, maintaining consummate professionalism, and fending off sudden attacks. In other words, I was focused on playing a solid defense. I didn't have time to be pissed off and, more truthfully, I couldn't afford to show such an emotion, so I just never allowed myself to feel it. That time was over.

Much like giving yourself permission to be selfish, giving yourself permission to be pissed off is a process unto itself, especially for women. We risk those labels. Bitch. Over-emotional. Irrational. High-maintenance. Complicated. The list goes on. It is never as simple as we've reached our threshold or even that we are passionate about something…we need to be labeled once we react, regardless of how valid our reaction may be. And God help you if you cry…ever.

The difference that happens when you actually get pissed off, though, is that your focus changes to being actionable rather than re-actionable. Instead of waiting and preparing for the next punch to be thrown, you begin acting in ways to stop the initial wind up from even happening. You do not show that you're pissed off, but you use that energy as fuel to *get in the fight and stay in the fight*. You begin to play phenomenal offense and that gives your defense just that little bit of space, that little break it needs. That little break that part of you needs.

So I became pissed off and stayed pissed off on that January night in 2019. Tired, beat down, tearful, frustrated, hurt, confused…absolutely…but all of those very real feelings never mattered after that moment because I was always pissed off and could find the energy in that to persevere. I've received so many compliments and questions throughout this whole crisis…how are you keeping it together? How do you maintain your composure? How do you keep doing your job? I could never do that.

Yes…you could. You just have to get pissed off.

And can I tell you a little secret? The more you learn to be pissed off and how to use that energy to add to your strength, the more you smile. And the more you smile, the more it pisses off your would-be kidnappers and other bad actors. And I have yet to meet even one of them who has ever put that extra energy to any good use. In fact, it normally causes them to implode.

Chapter 5
Strength

I often catch myself reflecting on events or times that seemingly don't have anything to do with each other but for some reason they are tied together in my head. Sometimes they are as simple as I remembered being at Myrtle Beach when I was around 5-years old and getting toppled over by a wave and in the same moment think of being in Mexico thirty years later and the same thing happening. Not too big of a stretch…me, sand, salt water and sun are in both memories so that link makes sense.

But others tend to be not so cut and dry. Like, I have a memory of my older brother and I, when I was maybe 10-years old, getting in trouble one night after our parents came home from dinner and we had left the kitchen a mess. We were sat down side-by-side in the kitchen and yelled at by our dad about being irresponsible and not taking it seriously that we were then finally allowed to even stay home alone. When that moment comes to mind, I also think of a manager I once had screaming her head off at me on the phone, crying even, about how stressful of a situation she was in because of a large account I managed with another employee that was going sideways. I was in the car, driving down the turnpike, and it was a woman yelling at me about work. Nothing to do with a kitchen, a father-figure, or dirty dishes…so what gives?

When I pause, though, I realize why they are related, even causal, in my mind. See, before my father entered the kitchen that night and my brother and I were in our kitchen-chair prison of silence, he leaned over to me and whispered, "Whatever he says, no matter how much he yells, don't react. If you don't react, he has nothing to keep yelling at us for and this will be over quicker." My brother was very wise at the age of 13.

When my manager was yelling at me on the phone, I did just what my brother had told me to do over 25 years ago: I didn't react when I was being yelled at. Granted, this person was like Stanley and so many other people that when she didn't get a reaction, it only enraged her more, but the basics were still the same as they were that night in my parent's kitchen: I wasn't giving her anything new to yell at me about so eventually we were left with her yelling and crying and me giving calm answers driving down the turnpike. The call ended quicker because that lesson was burnt in my brain. I didn't get in the van with her.

I find there are so many moments like that. Moments that are precursors to situations I have yet to encounter where I have learned to do or not do something that benefits me in a completely unrelated situation years later. And the ones that shock me aren't the obvious ones like the beach example or having dated that "hot, free-spirited guy who had such awesome ideas to be successful if he only went to bed once in a while before 2 am and got up before noon." Sure, there are those. But, for me, it's the ones where the correlation, and sometimes even what I learned, aren't outwardly obvious that grab hold of my attention. The ones that take me months or even years to say, "Ahh, so *that's* why I was able to do that…good one, Universe."

After a little bit more than a year in my current position, Stanley and I had what could only be categorized as a complicated working relationship. On one hand, he loved me because of the revenue I generated and the mutually beneficial C-suite relationships I fostered for our business unit. On the other hand, he hated me for those things and the attention they brought me if he couldn't find a way to claim part of the credit. I'll admit, it was probably tedious for both of us. When I could stomach it, I went out of my way to include him in the innerworkings of what I did, cc'ing him on emails to clients rather than forwarding them after the fact so he could add his thoughts to projects, and inviting him to C-suite appointments with me under the guise that I could really use his insights. It was and felt ridiculous to do, but it ultimately made our relationship at least a little bit less contentious. We went on that way for quite a while.

And then sometime during the end of my second year on his team, I guess Stanley had hit some kind of a threshold with the structure of our relationship. We had just hired a new sales rep in the in the southwest. I was close friends with the area sales manager there and had helped him with the interviews. I was thrilled with the woman he decided to hire and wanted to do anything I could to help her get off to a fast start. So, since one of her sales accounts was also one of my key accounts, I invited her to not only join me in my meetings one day, but also to carve out a few hours in the afternoon where I could essentially answer any questions she had, help her get set up remotely, and generally make her feel welcomed and excited about her new career.

We found space at a Starbucks to set up camp. She was eager, excited and came with tons of questions and ideas. As a woman who loves to be around open-minded, strong female professionals, I was over the moon. We had hired someone who was going to erase the pains of her marginal predecessor. Angels were singing in my head.

Somewhere around hour two of our session, the sales rep asked me if she could ask me something. That's why we were here, I thought, so of course. She then shyly, quietly blindsided me and said, "Why doesn't your boss like you? What's the problem?"

Even years later I find myself telling my then self to "just breathe" in that moment.

I was committed to fostering her excitement about her new position, but I have to admit that hellfire went through every inch of me when I heard those words. With all of the professionalism, fortitude, and compartmentalization I could muster, I calmly asked her what happened to make her feel something was wrong. She proceeded to tell me that a couple of days prior, she was with Stanley and her manager for a series of meetings in an account that had not been determined as a key target of mine. The account was located mere minutes away from one of my current account's locations that I met with monthly. Her manager told Stanley that he wanted me to take over the account and, it would simply make sense: I was already in the area frequently, I had solid relationships, and from a cost-effectiveness standpoint, it would give us more bang-for-our-buck on my travel expenses. Sounded like a good business idea all around to me.

However, per our new less-than-a-week-old sales rep and her manager who I confirmed the story with later, Stanley did not agree. In fact, he doubled-down on how that revenue-generating, cost-effective idea was never going to happen by announcing:

"Why do you keep bringing up Anslie's name to me? You're not going to get to work with her on anymore accounts out here. I'm sick of you and everyone else talking about her. You act like she's some kind of dynamo and she's really not. Stop asking me to have her partner with your team. It's not going to happen."

Any question I had in my head if the new sales rep misinterpreted this situation went right out the window. Yep…I'd probably have asked me why my boss didn't like me, too.

I did my best to do an instant regroup and explain to her that our business relationship was complicated, while trying to avoid saying anything that might make her regret her decision and think she accidentally joined a shitshow circus. Our onboarding session was completely derailed but I felt like I addressed her concerns while extinguishing the fire. Well, at least I didn't think I added fuel to the fire. Our afternoon ended a bit awkward but fine. When I jumped in my rental car, I immediately called my friend, her boss, where he confirmed the story she shared with me.

At this point I had a choice to make: pick up the phone and confront Stanley, which I had done previously with no change in any behaviors, or wait until we would be together in-person with his boss, Don, and speak to the two of them to eliminate any games of telephone. Since we were all to be at a meeting together later that week, I went with the latter option. Of course, since the universe cannot be on my side all of the time, I managed to be at a 3-day conference, never once getting an opportunity or being able to create an opportunity where Stanley, Don and I could grab 5 minutes for a private conversation. Now what? I live in the Midwest. Stanley lives in the southwest. Don lives out west. The chances of the three of us being in the same place again before the next management meeting was slim to null. On top of that it was the beginning of November, so the holidays were upon us.

But then, the universe decided to throw me a bone. Even though it was the early building blocks of my pit of despair laid out in front of me, more than 2 years before my crisis' grand opening, I didn't yet realize it at the time: for no given reason and with only a couple of days' notice for preparation, Stanley and Don were flying to my neck of the woods to have a formal business review with Hayden and me. No other area teams were being reviewed. Just us. I embraced the suck. This was a gift.

During this pre-crisis time Hayden and I had a decent working relationship. There were definitely significant differences in how we approached life, but all was workable. Not perfect, but what is? She had even on occasion shared with me that she felt discriminated against as only one of a small handful of female managers on her team. Being the only woman on my management team, we had a commonality, a small bond. It was based on that small bond that I shared with Hayden in advance of our business review that I was going to need to grab 5 minutes in private with Stanley and Don at the conclusion of it. I made sure to let her know that while I couldn't tell her what the meeting was about, the one-off had nothing to do with her or with us or anyone on our team. It was something specific to me and me alone. She, of course, tried to inquire, but in the end acquiesced and said that she would excuse herself to get her car on my cue.

At the conclusion of our business review in the lobby of an airport hotel, it went like this:

Me: "Hey, Don, Stanley…before you go, I'd like to grab a few minutes of your time."

Don: "Well, we have to get to the airport so we don't have a lot of time."

Me: "If I needed more than a few minutes, I wouldn't have waited until now."

(Don excuses himself to the bathroom)

Stanley: "What's this about? If there's something you need to talk to me about, just tell me."

Me: "No. I'll wait for Don to come back."

(Don returns and sits down laughing)

Don: "So, Anslie, what's going on? What do you need to talk to us about?"

Breathe. Just breathe.

Me: "Listen, at the end of the day I don't care what either of you personally think of me or if you even like me, I really don't. But what I do care about is that publicly we all present a united team to others."

Stanley/Don in unison uttered: "What are you talking about?"

Me: "A couple of months ago I was onboarding our new rep in the southwest when she asked me point blank why my boss didn't like me. She proceeded to tell me, Stanley, what you said about me to her and her boss when her boss asked for me to take over another account in his region."

Stanley: "No, no, no…I don't know what you are talking about. We had a discussion but there was nothing bad. I don't even remember what was said."

Me: "Well, I do. You said, "Why do you keep bringing up Anslie's name to me? You're not going to get to work with her on anymore accounts out here. I'm sick of you and everyone else talking about her. You act like she's some kind of dynamo and she's really not. Stop asking me to have her partner with your team. It's not going to happen.""""

Stanley/Don: "Things were taken out of context. Oh, no, that's not it. I'm sorry you were told that. You're fantastic. That didn't happen."

Me: "So is the new sales rep lying?"

Stanley: "No, no…it was just an emotional moment. I shouldn't have said that. There was a lot going on. Again, it was taken out of context."

Me: "Well, the only context that matters is what the new sales rep thinks and right now the new sales rep thinks that we have some major problems. She just got here, for God's sake. This situation completely derailed our meeting. So what I'm going to need from you is to be a little less emotional in the future since you're saying that was the problem. Can you do that?"

Stanley: "Again, I'm sorry. This shouldn't have happened. I'll call her and explain."

Me: "No, do not call her and put her on the spot."

Don then proceeded to make some snarky closing statement about me not being afraid of anything. Well, Donny Boy, I wouldn't go that far but I'm sure as shit not afraid of you two.

So that happened.

What ensued after that moment fortunately never included a call to a new sales rep from a leader several rungs up the ladder from her, but rather just a lot of immediate fake ass-kissing to me. The tiny handful of people I told about the incident who knew me, Don, and Stanley, giggled like teenage girls watching the latest TikTok or some Instagram Story. It *was* funny. I mean, women are supposed to be the emotional ones, right? And here I was, confronting 2 male national leaders of a multi-million-dollar business unit and one of them simply offered up that I was misunderstanding the moment in question…because he had been too emotional. I thought of all the times that so many women had been mislabeled as "too emotional" year after year and meeting after meeting and I smiled. I fucking smiled big.

But then, or sometime close to then, a few confidantes started using phrases that sounded more like "that took some serious guts" and "how did you do that" rather than "that was so awesome." Their comments caused me to pause. This wasn't the first time Stanley had made backhanded remarks about me, or even the tenth time for that matter. But this time was different…why? I had thought I just reached my breaking point with Stanley and his passive aggressive comments, but had I? I wasn't so sure when I really stopped and thought about it. I was uncomfortable with trying to figure out my end game with that situation for a long time. A very long time. So long that I stopped dissecting or even thinking about the situation because I started to lose the empowering feelings born of what I had done. They were being replaced with confusion and that pissed me off a bit.

It wasn't until nearly a year later that I understood what was different on that day in the hotel lobby with Stanley and Don. I was different. Yes, I had hit a breaking point. But, oddly enough, it was a strength point. Or rather I tapped into a strength I hadn't known I had, but I sure as hell knew I had it at a leadership meeting nearly 10 months later.

We were at a management meeting in 2018, less than a month after my discovery of Evan and Hayden's shady account, I-swear-its-not-a-kickback setup. Stanley had been playing defense and avoidance with me for a few weeks and I still didn't have an answer to my questions. In the meantime, Evan had been promoted to National Director and due to my geography responsibilities, I was about to inherit the said account with the shady practices. My inquiries had escalated from being solely concerned about the company to being concerned about myself as well. I couldn't knowingly walk into an unethical situation like that. And, furthermore, what the hell did they think I would do when anyone there asked me for help or advice? Sure, let me make you a PowerPoint detailing how better to break the law and bilk your customers? I'll laminate it for you so you can post it in the lunchroom. Fuck.

Stanley approached me at breakfast that morning, asking me if I was ok with the situation and the answers I received. When I told him I was not, he became noticeably agitated and asked me why. I explained that I hadn't heard he spoke to Legal or Compliance or the head of that free service's department and I couldn't imagine how they shouldn't be looped in. His answer? He talked to Evan and Hayden and they told him it was just a misunderstanding.

Well, I guess that just settles that then.

I shared with him that because I was set to inherit the account and no one had given me any answers, to verify my concerns I had spoken to a friend in the legal world. My friend shared with me that I should be worried about what I learned if I were going to take over the account because what I described was at best unethical and at worst highly illegal. The only thing more drastic than the look on Stanley's face was the way it felt like the air got sucked out of the room.

The morning of meetings proceeded uneventfully. After lunch our team was sent to a breakout room for a "Compliance presentation." Interestingly enough, no one from Compliance was in the room, but several members of my crisis' cast decided to attend.

For reasons unknown to me then but crystal clear now, Stanley chose to use as an example of non-compliant behavior something I set up for the participants in my soon-to-be-ill-fated leadership group. He called it an inducement and, even though as soon as I was told that we couldn't provide such a service I handed over the reins to one of the people in the group, proceeded to elaborate to everyone who from corporate had gotten involved, what happened to me (which was nothing), and the problems I could have caused for the company. Sitting in my seat quietly, I internally rolled my eyes at the unnecessary drama.

He moved onto what was supposedly his direction from Compliance to answer my ethical concerns. It was a joke. He was telling a group of professionals who directly work with C-Suites...mind you, with Don and Evan and a new Director who used to be a massive key client until our company hired her (let that soak in for a minute) in the room...to simply tell clients to check with their own operations department about any questions if we "hear or see anything that seems questionable." Oh, and that we should just document the encounter in our on-line files as "I told so-and-so to talk to their operations department." No need to talk to our Legal or Compliance department. No need to tell anyone. Don even chimed in at one point with some comment about acting like we are totally unfamiliar with what they're even talking about.

I decided to end whatever game of telephone was going on about this entire situation...*wait, I think I have been here before.*

I inhaled…I exhaled…and then this came out, "Stanley, I have got to be blunt with you and everyone else in here. If I am ever in a situation where a client asks me about bundling something inappropriately for customers or tells me that they are already conducting business in a way that I know to be inappropriate, I'm not simply telling them to talk to their operations department and I'm not going to act like I'm some idiot that doesn't understand. I'm telling them that what they are doing is unethical and likely illegal. Then I am getting in my car and calling our Legal department directly. That's my reputation and my integrity on the line, not to mention our company's."

Suffice to say, that didn't exactly go over well. There was discussion amongst the group, with a couple people openly agreeing with me which didn't help the growing tension in the room. Stanley continued trying to make his non-point with the support of the co-conspirators that were there. It was all disjointed and scrambling. When the meeting finally ended, Stanley et al stuck to the original script, though: deflect and document that you deflected. Period.

A bit later the general meeting wrapped up and people started the airport departure rideshare program. One of my friends and I did not have departures for a few hours so we chose to hang out and get some work done for a bit with plans to leave for the airport later. As we chatted, Stanley came up and told me that he and Don wanted to catch up with me for a few minutes.

We walked out into the hallway. He gestured for me to follow him down the hall. He pointed to a meeting room. Don was seated there. I walked in. Stanley walked in behind me and shut the door. They both sat across from me.

Ahhhhhh, I have been here before. This should be interesting.

Don and Stanley had collectively decided that I needed to be talked to and apparently that talk needed to happen locked in a room alone with the two of them. When I joked that it felt like I was being taken out to the woodshed before I sat down, they both laughed, said no and for me to have a seat. It was clear to me that the woodshed was exactly where they wanted me to feel like I was.

Over the next 15 minutes or so, they hit all the dog whistling high points: trust issues, I misunderstood the situation, I was part of a team, we had to work together, Hayden misspoke…the list goes on. It was a playback of every initial response to every corporate whistleblower in history. And the smugness that they had…that smugness that they caught me off guard and I would crack under their pressure or even possibly apologize was so evident that it was palpable. But that smugness…*I had been here before. Exactly here.*

One of the most memorable points for me in the room that day went something like this:

Don and Stanley spoke for several minutes but the gist of all of their many words was, "We don't feel you believe in us. You seem mistrustful."

When I replied with my tenth, "I'm sorry? What?" Stanley quite simply stated, "The situation you brought up." I tried to muster all possible respect when I stated, "Well, you haven't answered my questions. I'm to take that account over. I'm concerned."

With a whisper of a pause and almost in unison they replied, "We did answer your questions and we spoke to Compliance and Legal."

"I find it hard to believe that Legal or Compliance wants us to look the other way." I couldn't believe what I was hearing.

Then…bam. Without warning a "Why did you talk to a lawyer?" flew through the air.

There went that breath caught in my throat again, "Excuse me?"

Stanley was all in on this one…Don was next to him. He actually smiled when he said, "Why did you feel the need to talk to a lawyer?"

Ok…here we go. Game on. "I didn't talk to a lawyer. I talked to a friend in the legal field," came out of my mouth with what I felt was a blank but pointed stare across the table.

All that I received in return was a "Well, whatever. Still, you involved an outsider and that's what we are talking about. If you trusted us, you wouldn't have done that. We told you we had it handled." Clearly, they felt shutdown procedures had begun.

As I attempted to shut whatever this shit was down with, "Well, you handled it for you and the company, not for me. I needed to speak to someone who was objective and uninvolved," they clearly wanted to keep digging when they said, "We are looking out for you. How can you say we are not?"

Days later I was told that the would-be-Dateline-Special account I was to inherit, the account that had had a manager like me for my entire tenure, now suddenly no longer needed one. I was not getting the account.

A few months later I learned from a Compliance Director that an attorney from our Legal department came to him and apologized. After receiving all of my information on the unethical matter, the attorney realized Stanley had lied to him about the actual scope of the situation, causing the attorney to give direction and advice that was not appropriate.

Shortly after the attorney's epiphany, the main customer contact who led the unethical situation on site was fired from his position, but then miraculously remained a paid consultant for our business unit with strong support from Stanley and Evan.

And then, almost immediately after his firing, I was unexpectedly brought into the account that was now in shambles from not having a management lead for so long.

I'm guessing that about sums up how I could say you were not looking out for me that day in the woodshed, guys.

I can still remember as clear as day both of those moments…that day at the airport hotel with Don and Stanley, asking Stanley to be less emotional in the future…and that day in the meeting hotel with Don and Stanley, being told I didn't trust them in spite of how much they were looking out for me. It's eerie when I think about those days side-by-side and their similarities. It's eerie but, oddly enough, it also fills me with inspiration, especially now that I've had so much time to think about it while I'm breathing this rare air.

In spite of what has turned into one of the most horrific professional situations I've personally heard of or experienced, I have continued to learn. I have continued to grow. I have gotten *stronger*.

That cold winter day at the airport hotel I had no idea the foundation I created for my future self, no idea how much inner strength I tapped into that I didn't know existed. People have always commented that I am a strong person, very focused and outspoken, which I am, but this strength was different…very different. I would liken it more that day to an *inner calm*. This feeling that the situation was in slow motion, or at least at a pace that I had some sort of control over. At the time I probably would have said that I felt in control the day at the airport hotel because I triggered the interaction and caught those two men off guard but years later I realize that wasn't the case at all. I felt in control of the moment because I was in complete control of myself, regardless of the reactions or actions of anyone else around me…just like that day a year later with Stanley and Don in the meeting hotel.

I can't overstate how many times throughout the ebb and flow of my crisis I have thought about those two events and not only the impact the interactions themselves had on me, but also the impact of being able to leverage that strength…that inner calm…in me that I didn't know I had. What an incredible gift to be able to open again and again and again.

These days I think there's probably a correlation from the 10-year-old me in the kitchen chair, learning to keep my mouth shut in certain moments, and the 40-something me, learning about her inner calm. They feel like they are different points on the same pathway to me.

I do that a lot lately, trying to uncover relationships between experiences I have had or behaviors I possessed at different points in life. At times I find doing so entertaining, but mostly I find spending time on such an introspective activity hugely beneficial. I would recommend it to anyone. Not only do you get the opportunity to laugh and remember the younger, less experienced you, but also you get to revel at how much you have grown, how much you have learned, and *how you became* the incredible and strong person you are today. The activity makes you start looking at other people differently, too, wondering about their journey, wondering how they became who they are, and wondering what previous experience they have had that is contributing to your experience with them today.

Chapter 6
You Never Know

That phrase "you never know" has become somewhat of a silent anthem for me over the last few years. You never know how someone will react. You never know what impact you are having on others. You never know how strong you are. You never know what tomorrow has in store. You never know if you will ever again have such an opportunity to demand change.

You never know what other people are going through.

You really don't. I am a living, walking posterchild of the fact that you don't…before, now, then, ever. The small amount of people who know about my crisis have told me dozens of times that if they didn't know what I was going through they would never know. That they don't understand how I manage or succeed or travel with my crisis' cast members or give them praises or whatever, all with a smile on my face and a spring in my step. Since I can't briefly overview how it's a combination of inner calm, learning to breathe and being permanently pissed off because they'd think I finally rounded the bend if I just rattled that recipe off, I just keep going.

Similarly over these more than five months of being mysteriously gone from my job and equally mysteriously home all of the time in spite of some business travel opening up again, people have no idea what I'm going through. I can't explain to my neighbors why I am here, or in my clients' cases, not there. I cannot tell them anything because, quite frankly, I cannot tell them anything. I am not allowed. So I smile and garden and workout and help out where I can and have little socially distant cocktail hours on the porch like everything is normal.

Because you never know what other people are going through.

At the beginning of 2019, I was in Orlando with my team for a management meeting. As you now know, my crisis and its cast members were just hitting their stride after a long holiday break. All of them were at this meeting so I was teetering between the joys of trying not to walk anywhere alone, making sure my pocket recorder was always handy and being extraordinarily put-together and professional every moment I was not in my hotel room. In retrospect, it was probably more of a thread than a tightrope I was walking on, but I didn't have any *rare air* to breathe then so I really didn't have time to think about it. I just kept moving.

One of my closest friends, Christopher, had been periodically excusing himself throughout the meeting to take phone calls. He didn't normally do this so after maybe the third time, I asked him on a break if he was ok. His grandfather, who had been in very poor but relatively stable health, had taken a turn for the worse. He was trying to work with his wife who was four hours away from his grandfather and his aunt, who was significantly closer but estranged from her dad, to obtain information and give input. It would be a lot on any day let alone on one where you are 1500 miles away in a room with colleagues and leaders of your company. Other than taking the phone calls, Christopher never missed a beat.

You never know what other people are going through.

At some point during the day, Christopher alerted Stanley to what was going on to avoid seeming disruptive to the meeting. So, late in the afternoon when a corporate leader was presenting to us with Don in the room and Christopher excused himself, Stanley didn't even blink. Nor did he blink several minutes later when Christopher returned to the room, holding back tears, to grab his things and leave. He didn't even so much as pause the meeting. Or better yet just be human and follow his employee out of the room to give him whatever support he needed in that moment.

Christopher's grandfather had died. I knew it. Stanley and Don knew it. Hell, anyone in the room knew something devastating had happened. In that moment, Stanley, Don, and I all knew what another person was going through.

I stared across the conference table at Stanley and Don, willing one of these leaders, our bosses, to move. To do something that hinted at empathy for someone they have both known for years.

Again, no one even blinked let alone stood up. The presenter simply continued speaking.

I shook my head, got up and walked out of the room to find Christopher. He was standing outside the meeting room door texting someone. We made eye contact and all I could do was hug him. We sat down and talked. I asked him what he needed and what he didn't need so I could either take care of things or run interference for him, telling him that I was having a one-off dinner with a mutual friend of ours that night and that he was welcome to join us if he wanted company to talk, or not talk at all. We were there for him. I have no idea how long we sat on that bench but it was awhile and no one ever came out to check on anything. Or anyone.

Christopher left for his room and I returned to the meeting. I don't know what I expected at that point but at the very least I think maybe a "Is Christopher ok?" would have been minimally appropriate. But again, nothing.

When the meeting ended and neither Stanley nor Don so much had made a single inquiry, I let everyone know what had happened. I choked up when I told them about Christopher's grandfather. Only then did Stanley make a comment that he should take Christopher out to dinner that night. The mama bear jumped right out of me and onto the conference table…no, but thanks…I have that covered…in my head all the while yelling, "your selfish ass who can't go actually be a friend to someone but who wants to pose as one in front of others to get those fake compassion credits...I don't think so. Not today."

A small, tightknit group of us hung out with Christopher that night before his o-dawn-thirty flight the next day. I saw Stanley at breakfast the next morning and he asked me how Christopher was and when he was leaving. Christopher was distraught and he was already inflight by this time. The only thing that ran through my mind in that instant was, "How on earth do you not know the answer to either of those questions? You're his fucking boss." Of course, I simply smiled and said he was ok and on his way home.

Our team convened after breakfast for our morning sessions that were to conclude for noon departures to the airport…remember that because it will come back around in a few minutes. By this time there were two other women besides me on the team. And while I don't think at that moment any of us had a complete relationship with each other, we did have a natural bit of camaraderie. So when we arrived and Stanley, without provocation, started berating one of them in front of me, I immediately locked in. He started referring to a presentation from the day before about emptying your cup so that you could learn and be open to new ideas…maintaining a full cup keeps you closed-minded and unwilling to learn. Whatever. The point is my colleague was just sitting there, the meeting hadn't even started. My guess is that like a lot of us, she has a resting bitch face sometimes and that was Stanley's trigger because I was sitting right next to her and can attest that she hadn't said a single word before he laid into her. Her cup was too full. She needed to empty her cup. She needed to refill her cup. Jesus, him and this stupid cup.

Suffice to say she handled herself just fine. She didn't get in the van. She told him she had no idea what he was talking about and that she was open to new ideas. Sounded like enough said to me. But she also didn't falsely turn a million-dollar smile on afterwards and now she was sitting right across from

Stanley for the duration of the meeting. Remember from before…Stanley becomes derailed when someone either doesn't react to his emotions or reacts in a way that doesn't mirror his emotions. For the next couple of hours he was sitting across from two women who had collectively done both in less than 30 days…me during my disciplinary plan call and my colleague 5 minutes ago. In retrospect it was inevitable that something was bound to implode. It was like leaving a kid with a book of matches and a box of fireworks.

You never know what someone else is going through.

With a little less than 30 minutes left before our noon departures for the airport, Stanley blurts out, "OK, I'm going to call an audible here."

We all just looked at each other with pained eyes…now what? And more importantly, whatever *this* was, we better not be missing our flights for it.

Stanley said that he was going to leave the room so we could essentially do an impromptu, informal assessment of him. Regarding his specific behaviors, he recommended we do the exercise in a STOP, START, CONTINUE format. We could take as long as we wanted. He would be waiting outside the door. When we were finished, we could then go out and get him, at which point he requested a couple of us to stay with him to go over the feedback immediately while the rest of us departed for the airport.

No preparation time, no knowledge that we were even going to do this exercise, and 25 minutes before most of us had to leave for the airport due to flight times. Yeah, my initial feedback was "this is total bullshit." Was he serious?

Sure enough he was serious because off he went. The five of us remaining just stared at each other for a minute stunned. We then tossed around what we should do, how specific we should be, what trouble simply doing this at all was going to cause for us with him. This was not the way for us to end an already too-long meeting. This was definitely not what I needed to be part of at the moment, that's for certain.

We collectively decided that no matter what we did or said or wrote, Stanley was going to overreact and not take it well. With that said, we agreed that we should be direct and specific in our answers and avoid sugar coating anything. Shit, if we were going to take a beating anyway, we may as well have our voices heard.

You never know what other people are going through.

That's when it happened. Someone brought up Stanley's passive aggressive nature for discussion. Clearly the most immediate example was the 'cup' incident from earlier that morning. Everyone agreed that it was blatant and unnecessary and, let's face it, weird. As we were talking, my other female colleague who had been pretty quiet in those first few minutes, chimed in.

She had a story.

As she began to talk tears welled up in her eyes. I didn't know what she was going to say but I knew the feelings that cause that type of reaction in a female business professional. It broke my heart for her. For me. For my other colleague earlier that morning. I didn't even know what she was going to say yet and I choked up.

Our fiscal year runs June to May, so our mid-year reviews occur in the December-January timeframe. She had had her mid-year review right before the holidays. Stanley was pretty harsh on her, but her numbers weren't where they needed to be, so she admitted she wasn't surprised by his tone. She began to explain to him what she felt would help her to succeed moving forward, things like more one-on-one time, demonstration of certain expected activities in action, specific software tutorials. She just needed training. In so many words, he told her she had to figure it out herself. We all stared at her because he had written a similar phrase on a flipchart the day before during one of our sessions, causing all of us to take pictures of it for later proof of his erratic, unhelpful behavior.

It was the next thing she said that took the air out of the room, though. Following Stanley telling her that she was on her own to figure out the position, she told us he then said something like this to her:

"Your numbers were the worst on the team this quarter. It's because of you that I don't have the money I need for Christmas gifts and other things for my wife and sons. Both of my sons are getting ready for college, too, so we need that money. It's your fault that I don't have it. You need to improve."

We were speechless. She was crying. As an equal breadwinner in her household, she, too, did not get to have the Christmas with her child that she would have liked. She, too, did not contribute as much to the family income as she typically did. She felt deflated by her own personal impact alone without her director blaming her for his household's finances, too. What an immense weight to have set on top of someone. How helpless and guilty she had to feel…and during a performance review, no less.

In that moment all I could do was reach for her hand and tell her how sorry I was that she had that horrible experience. All of us chimed in with understanding and support, offering to help her in the areas where she wanted to improve and sharing that in different ways we had all been subject to Stanley's negative behaviors. I told her that it wasn't worth me getting into at that moment but for her to please know that I understood what she was feeling…I really did. She could call me anytime.

Those of us who had to leave did, with a couple of our colleagues staying behind to deliver the feedback we had compiled. In spite of my high comfort level with speaking truth to power, I didn't envy not being the one to do it that day. I was exhausted in every aspect of the word and just wanted to get the hell home, or at least away at that point. Far, far away.

At the airport I met with one of my colleagues who delivered the feedback to Stanley. She said she didn't really know how to explain what happened which sounded strange to me. It was feedback, and pretty cut and dry feedback at that. What could be hard to explain?

In all of the times I've ever been part of a feedback session, I can't recall a single instance where the person broke down in sobbing tears when they received the feedback but that's apparently what happened when they spoke to Stanley. Giving feedback to your boss and he starts crying? OK, now I saw how this might be hard to explain.

Per my colleague, they began to go through the STOP, START, CONTINUE grid that we completed, where we included specific examples of each behavior to help focus the discussion. They didn't get but a couple minutes into the session when Stanley became agitated, buried his head in his hands and started openly crying. I asked her what they did when it happened. She kind of laughed and said they started to try to smooth over the impact while still giving the feedback, but it was somewhat disjointed because of, you know, the crying. As I listened then and think about it now, I am left to still wonder if Stanley was using the breakdown as a diversion to avoid having the serious discussion he had requested or if he was a raw nerve because he was being tied to all of the negative situations I brought to light or if he was dealing with something else entirely.

You never know what other people are going through.

It might be hard for someone to imagine me being able to show empathy at this point to someone like Stanley after all that has happened, all the detriment he has been part of in my life. I'll be honest: I didn't have much empathy for him that day.

But in the many months since that day in Orlando and especially in these last five months I have had plenty of time to think about different interactions I have had…both those that were amazing and those that were devastating. And, as you know, with time often comes a different perspective and my perspective on that day has certainly changed.

I was left to ask myself one question: If no one in that room knew what I was going through, and I didn't know what Christopher or either of my two female colleagues were going through, how could I also not recognize that Stanley was likely going through something I didn't know about, too? How could I not factor that into the equation of that day? The answer was simple. I couldn't.

While I can't go back to that day, inject my new perspective and change anything, I can use it moving forward. I have used it moving forward from communicating with my family to talking with friends who seem agitated to talking with my attorney. Everyone is going through something *all of the* time and I now try to keep that permanently in mind, no matter what I am going through myself. I have found new, indirect ways to ask the person I am talking to if they are alright or if they'd like to talk about something else on their mind, and I continue to improve being silently empathetic when my words could ring false or invasive or simply just weird.

Listen, I still do not agree with how Stanley and many other cast members have treated me and some of my peers and I never will. I do not think they are well-intended towards anything or anyone other than protecting their secrets and staying out of the truth that sunlight brings. That's unfortunately a hard fact. But they are all going through something that I don't know about and that has to mean something. It could mean that there are opportunities for me to better understand. It could mean conversations and mediations might be more fruitful if I asked different questions. It could mean that I learn a new perspective that helps me eventually achieve my end game.

Chapter 7
End Games

I have this friend who used to ask me at every point in my crisis, "How much money do you think this is worth?" And every time she did, I gave her the same response: I have no idea. That's not what this is about. It's about getting bad behaviors to stop. But she would persist and wonder aloud and seemingly find new ways to ask me the same thing, trying to get me to engage. She would tell me about random, related topics she googled and send me stories of corporate harassment cases as though she was helping me in some way. This odd Q&A scenario went on for months and then escalated when I finally filed with the EEOC. Her questions got more specific, almost invasive, asking about conversations with my attorney and what his experiences had been with cases like mine. Making suppositions about why she felt I should get *this* or why I should be demanding *that*. And still my answer remained the same: I have no idea. That's not what this is about. It's about getting bad behaviors to stop.

Finally one day I had to shut down her line of questioning all together…I only had so much RAM and I couldn't afford to keep wasting any of what I had on these questions that I found highly annoying, not to mention would never answer no matter how many times she asked. After I gave her my standard answer one last time, I added this:

"Listen, you really need to stop asking me about money because I am never going to answer you. In fact, you're the only friend I have whoever asks me about the money aspect at all. However this situation finally resolves, the only person in my world who is going to know anything specific is my attorney, not you. So please drop it or I'm not going to be able to talk to you anymore about the situation."

But here is my question: With so many devastating, and sometimes intriguing, components of my crisis, why did she keep primarily asking me about money? Why, after months of me deliberately not answering her questions, did I have to state something so blunt, so obvious to her?

I didn't have the answer then, but I do now…in this *rare air*. Quite simply put, money was *her* end game. Not her end game for my crisis, but rather her end game for her personally…for her own life. *It was what she needed* so no matter what I said, she felt it must be what I ultimately needed as well. I believe in my heart that she was not ill-intended in her inquiries and there's also nothing wrong with having money as an end game. Where things become murky and communications tend to break down is when someone either assumes or forces their end game on someone else: this is what is most important to me so it must be what is most important to you. I see that that was happening plain as day now and laugh at myself that I couldn't see it then.

Having money solved my friend's problems or helped her deal with her problems or somehow just made things better for her. It was what she needed. Her overall lifestyle had a tremendous focus on not only having a lot of money but doing things that showed she had a lot of money. So when we would have these conversations that I found disjointed it's because they were disjointed. We weren't just on different playing fields. We were playing completely different sports. We had different life end games.

Even though, as I said, there is nothing wrong with having money as an end game, I guarantee my friend wouldn't state that money was her life's end game. We previously discussed how most people can't articulate their end games either because they don't know them, or they've decided it's something else, something softer and more politically correct. Something that sounds better. I believe that's what my friend would do. For instance, "money is my end game" doesn't really have as nice of a ring to it as "I want to be a good provider to my family." While one sentiment can definitely be impacted by the other, they're not interchangeable…they don't mean the same thing.

When I think back to my friend's questions and those subsequent conversations that took place, the theme is crystal clear to me now. Her life end game was staring me in the face, and I just didn't see it, or maybe didn't want to see it. Maybe I internally *did* have a problem with money being a focal point. Not for her, but for me. Each time I think through this scenario I arrive at a wider understanding of it and myself which I find tremendously helpful to this journey. How many other peoples' end games had I overlooked or chosen not to see? And what impact has that had on my crisis and on the rest of my life?

Recognizing someone else's end game is incredibly important. However, as important as I have concluded that it is, I have found making sure I know and understand my own end game in every situation to be far more important. In fact, it may be the single most critical factor to my professional and personal success, as well as my overall happiness.

What is it that I actually need from my crisis? Not *what do I want*. But what do I really need to have happen for me to be satisfied, for me to succeed, for me to move on?

A few months ago my attorney and I participated in preliminary discussions with my company. By this time he and I knew each other pretty well. We had talked often about what I ideally wanted to have happen and why. I loved my job when I actually got to do it. I loved my clients and their customers I supported. I even loved my company…just not the situation I was in, making my decision to file a claim against them an even harder decision for me. So when my attorney sat me down to review options to move forward, I was pleased to see that the first option he wanted to discuss was to remove the bad actors and make me whole again by giving me my job back, not give me some huge sum of money. He explained and I understood that the first option was highly unlikely to happen even though it would be the rightest action for them to take. But, nonetheless, I felt at least the other people who were now involved in my situation would hopefully catch a glimpse of my true intentions, my end game: I wanted bad behaviors that were hurting people to stop.

Sometime after those preliminary discussions, an individual involved in the situation suggested to my company that due to the character and integrity that he believed I had, and the proof I had provided, they should consider an "unconventional" resolution. In other words, they should find a way to return me to work and remove the bad actors. They, unfortunately, didn't see or didn't care or, more than likely, just couldn't believe that I really didn't want it to come down to money if it didn't have to, or that I truly only wanted bad behaviors to stop, because here I sit with my crisis now rounding out six months of administrative leave. To add a new fun fact into the equation, a few months ago I transitioned from paid to unpaid leave…sit with that thought for a few minutes.

Anyway, since that last conversation, my company moved from conducting their own internal investigation to hiring a firm to do an unbiased external investigation into these bad behaviors I'm claiming occurred. I asked my attorney if he thought they hired this firm just to provide an image of impartiality or because they actually found proof of my claims and realized due to all involved that they couldn't conduct the investigation on their own. He told me that we would never know but it was likely a combination of both. I couldn't help but wonder how all of these twists and turns, how having a non-cast member now running the investigation, was impacting everyone's end game…especially when I was quite certain they were hoping all of those delays and changes would negatively impact mine. I mean, think about it…no salary, no insurance, no communications with anyone. I had to break soon, right?

Suffice to say, regardless of the investigation's findings, I am not getting my job back and that's ok. Friends and family who have heard me for two years state that if I lost my job over this, I'd be ok, have recently begun re-asking me. It's as though they thought in theory I would be fine, or that I thought in theory I would be fine, but maybe I hadn't really grasped the reality of what it meant to follow this through? I don't know. But what I do know and what I continue to tell them is that I am very much, very wholly ok… I planned for this phase of my crisis to happen a long time ago. And remember…keeping my job wasn't my end game any more than receiving financial benefits.

Making a change, forcing the elimination of bad behaviors that were hurting employees, clients and their customers was and always had been my end game. That's what I needed to move on. That's what I *need* to move on.

These days, now that I am not running a thousand miles per hour, I catch myself ruminating on certain points of time in my crisis where I can now see my end game peeped its head out to see how I was doing. These inflection points, these moments where things changed either subtly or blatantly, that I didn't realize at the time were proof all along that I was always seeking and striving for change, capture my attention and curiosity. One of those moments that I reflect upon often was the timeframe in the spring of 2019.

By mid-March, my disciplinary action was officially over. I had satisfied all the requirements and then some. Stanley, reluctantly as I learned from Rachel, scheduled a call with me to close out the situation. I remember being so prepared and ready for a major discussion, feeling at least a sense of relief that this would finally be behind me. When Stanley did not even spend 15 minutes speaking to me about it, I was shocked bordering on insulted. But then again, when I thought about it, what could he say? I was ranked number one on the team and had satisfied all the bogus requirements he threw at me. He managed to sound magnanimous about my success, as if him putting me on the disciplinary plan had somehow created a new, amazing set of capabilities in me. He gave me a few short remarks about making sure I learned from the experience, but that was it. We hung up and I just sat in my current hotel room and stared at the phone.

That's when it hit me. I was still here.

He hadn't achieved *his* end game. *Their end game.* For over six months he and his fellow cast members had been trying to get me fired or get me to quit and nothing had worked. Even though I laughed out loud in that moment in March, I realized that my crisis was not over just because I had survived those six months. I was likely only experiencing a delay of game while they revisited their playbook. Shit.

Over the next week not only did our team attend an impromptu, mandatory and workshop with Stanley, but we were also all interviewed by one of our female executives, Karen. Karen had apparently been read into my situation and my other colleagues' complaints against Stanley by Compliance and another former executive before he left the company. Karen claimed to want to do right by her employees so she engaged my close friend, Christopher, and I to round up the troops, tell them she and Compliance would like to have candid conversations with everyone, and that every conversation would be confidential, contributing to a change that was clearly needed. In other words, they could safely speak without worry of repercussions.

Christopher and I discussed the situation and agreed we had to do something. Christopher wanted the environment to change for the better, too. He had the same belief in the company as I did. We shared similar life end games. We split the list of colleagues and reached out to everyone, encouraging them to speak up. From what we learned, everyone was candid. Everyone spoke up. Everyone wanted change. And Karen promised each and every person the same thing: she was going to rectify the situation and make our environment safe and free from harassment and retaliation immediately.

I remember sitting in that workshop looking at Stanley and just hoping that the pain he had caused me and attempts he had made to disparage my reputation were finally going to be addressed. *The bad behaviors were going to stop.* Even when he came up to hug me like we were somehow friends or in any way on good terms, I smiled on the inside. He hadn't broken me, and the karma train was going to be pulling into his station momentarily. My colleagues and I were making a difference.

We heard through the grapevine that Stanley was sat down by some sort of executive team. Several people then received invitations to provide formal feedback on Stanley from an outside vendor where everyone doubled down on what they shared in the Karen interviews. Men. Women. Tenured and new…everyone stood up. I then heard from Rachel that HR and relevant leadership were addressing the issues with Stanley directly and in an actionable format. To say at that point that everyone who participated was on bated breath would be an immeasurable understatement.

And then weeks went by…and we heard nothing.

We heard nothing from Stanley. We heard nothing from HR. We heard nothing from Karen. People who I had encouraged to speak up began calling me, expressing overwhelming anxiety every time the phone rang and it was Stanley or Don or Evan because they had disclosed bad behaviors on all of them…were they calling to confront their accuser? Did they even know what they had been accused of? Every call, every interaction with these bad actors was being fretted over and scrutinized. In a matter of weeks our unified front to force change and speak truth to power had become a skeleton of itself. Everyone was walking on eggshells, and no one had any answers.

Since I was essentially the Firestarter of this situation, I called Compliance to ask what the hell was going on and to share with them the anxiety that had taken over about a dozen high-performing professionals' lives in the organization. The Compliance officers were confused. What did I mean no one had spoken to us? They had instructed Karen not even once, but three times, to address everyone who came forward to provide closure to the situation and explain any next steps. Well, I said, it appears as though Karen didn't feel you gave her direction so much as a mere suggestion to consider because she hasn't said boo to any of us.

I asked if it would be appropriate for me to request a follow-up call with her and the Compliance officers agreed doing so was very appropriate. I can't help but wonder now if they were so onboard with the idea because I was essentially a living, breathing I-told-you-so that they could throw to Karen later when she inevitably would have to tell them about our call.

I requested a meeting with Karen and on one spring evening that conference call took place. I'd like to say I was pleasantly surprised. I'd like to say it went well and I felt heard. I'd like to say that I didn't think anyone else was in the room with her, coaching her to repeat the same politically correct phrase to me over and over again. I'd like to tell you that it didn't end with me telling her that I knew what she knew and also that she wasn't doing a god damn thing about it. I'd love to say that I told her I felt safe and that so much had changed and everyone was thrilled they had broken their silence.

Yeah, I wish I could say all of those things but it wouldn't be true. I hung up the phone and just stared at it like I did after my conclusion call with Stanley a month prior.

What was true, though, was within a week I received a meeting request from Doris, the Senior HR Director, to "catch up because she felt out of the loop." I thought to myself that that was such a clever way to word that one of the highest-ranking executives of the company told you that she had a complicated call with me a few nights ago and there was a problem.

I was the problem. Still.

I was still here, meaning not only was their end game not complete, but based on my call with Karen, I wasn't knocked down at all from their previous nefarious efforts. I was still very much in the fight. And that fact was a real fucking problem for Karen because she was a key decision maker of my business unit when the unethical business situation was setup. The proverbial buck stopped with her. She knew it and she knew that I knew it, too.

A few days later I had the "catch up" call with Rachel and Doris. I asked them right out of the gate if we were talking because they had spoken to Karen. The short answer was yes. The long answer was the better part of an hour on the phone while I sat in a teeny tiny airport, staring at travelers, wondering if any of their professional lives were as fucked up as mine was at that moment.

Over the course of that hour, I answered all their questions and learned much to my utter disgust, that while Stanley had been addressed and given some corrective direction of sorts, nothing was really going to happen to him because…wait for it…*they had to give him an opportunity to change*. And as for all of the compelling, leave-yourself-out-on-a-limb information my colleagues and I had shared with Karen? Yeah, Rachel and Doris had only received maybe a third of it. Most of what I was telling them they were hearing for the first time. I thought for a moment they were faking their confusion and shocked pauses, but no. They were blindsided. I even asked them. They shared that learning this information now certainly didn't make their lives easier in any way. Wow. It doesn't? That must suck. I can't imagine.

I was simultaneously infuriated and disheartened. Every one of those cast members was either covering for someone, covering for themselves, creating plausible deniability, or simply not engaging because, let's face it, after the Compliance and HR people saw what happened to me, they sure as hell didn't want to formally cross any of the other cast members. It wasn't good and they knew it.

I could only end the call by restating for the umpteenth time that I remained in a horrific environment and that nothing had changed for me or anyone else. For the third time in recent weeks I was left staring stupefied at my phone. What was going on with these people? It was like they were all part of some creepy cabal.

And what about my end game? What about that change, that difference I needed to see? As beat down as I recall feeling in that moment, I can almost still feel how thoroughly pissed off I was at the same time. It was palpable. Like I told you before, I got pissed off mid-January in that dark, cold hotel parking lot and I stayed pissed off.

This was wrong. All of it. What they'd done to me. How they encouraged Christopher and I to recruit others to attest who were now out there feeling exposed and vulnerable. How they promised change and improvement and a commitment to their employees and did nothing. I couldn't believe it then any more than I can believe it now.

Over those next couple of weeks Stanley talked to each of us about his formal feedback and employees had to attend a mandatory virtual Harassment in the Workplace seminar, both instances served up as some kind of potential closure or awareness for those of us affected by everything. But both were a joke. Stanley, who received the most comprehensive, scathing feedback from a large group of people I'd ever heard of, likened it to "us not telling him that he was walking around with a booger hanging out of his nose." Yeah, so those conversations clearly aren't worth wasting time to discuss. And the seminar? I got Rachel to send me the recording of it. I forwarded it to my attorney. I laughed because I had followed the guidelines they presented to the letter and continued to be royally screwed. He laughed because it was such a bush league presentation and set of guidelines in the first place for a corporation of any size, let alone one of our caliber.

It then became a weird, oddly quiet time that Spring. My disciplinary plan was well in the rearview, but nothing had changed. Stanley and the other cast members had been called out by multiple, credible people and nothing had changed. Stanley momentarily let up on his passive aggressive behaviors but replaced them with over-compensating in other areas to show whatever it was he was hoping to show to senior leadership. Annoying, and again, nothing had changed. But it was quiet.

I was still there, trying to figure out how to reach my end game, starting to worry that no one would ever be held accountable. As big of a problem as that was for me, I quickly learned it was an even bigger problem for the people I was up against. That weird, odd quietness I was feeling that Spring should have been a red flag for me. I should have thought back to when I was a kid and my mom would suddenly pop her head into my room and say, "Oh, ok. You're ok. It was just too quiet back here so I had to check to see what you were up to."

It was too quiet. I should have checked to see what they were up to because they hadn't reached their end game yet either. I should have known that they were not as patient in reaching their end game as I was in reaching mine. I should have known something was coming.

Remember how I said that our fiscal year runs June to May? By this time we were well into the fourth quarter of our year. I was running a close race for first place with one of my good friends, but I was currently the frontrunner with only a few weeks to go. Being first meant Gold Circle. And Gold Circle meant a pretty badass trip, some extra bonus money and a few other cool things. I have to be honest after the year I'd had, that wouldn't suck.

Out of nowhere Stanley told us that there had been a change to the regional alignment…but not really a change…more of a clarification. A regional alignment "clarification" in the fourth quarter? This should be interesting.

One change that had been implemented at the *beginning* of that fiscal year related to where our team supported sales efforts across the country. Think of an "all-hands-on-deck" mentality…*we don't have the ratio that we ideally want so we're going to need everyone to pitch in.* The short end of the story was those of us that were in the role at the beginning of the year were asked to travel more extensively and learn more markets to support the business unit until we were fully staffed. Not a great ask of already stretched road warriors but there were incentives: notable commissions and whatever sales we supported would feed into our year-end totals, regardless of where the support occurred relative to our designated geography. By the end of the year this was significant since not only was I the only manager with long-term, continued support in a few accounts that were technically no longer under my purview, but I was also running such a close race with my colleague. This pain-in-the-ass ask had turned into a little pocket of joy for me.

This realignment component was what Stanley wanted to offer clarification on with only a handful of weeks left in the fiscal year.

He stated that some combination of himself, Don, Evan, and Operations had decided that they weren't going to include any of those out-of-region orders and efforts past the 2nd quarter of the year in our total generated revenue for the year. He claimed it had something to do with an inability of operations to calculate proper credit which, if you know anything about operations and the type of internal alignment in question, would have zippo to do with anything. Any orders related to those realignments that were fulfilled after the second quarter were null to our bottom line and null to our year-end ranks.

What. The. Fuck.

Remember me saying that the race I was in was tight? Remember me saying I was the only manager with existing outside-of-region clients?

I told you I thought they were some creepy cabal.

With only a few weeks left in the year, they managed to get approved a change to the aligned revenues that literally only impacted me. The change removed thousands of dollars from my annual revenue achievement but not a dime from anyone else's. When I protested to leadership, no one even batted an eye, stating that they never claimed any specific revenue alignment structure at the beginning of the year. When I protested again and inquired why would have I continued to travel all over the country outside of my region or spent the dozens of hours it took to secure and implement these client relationships if nothing was set in stone, the cast members simply stated I must have misheard things. Later, Don went so far as to say to me he couldn't comment on a private conversation I may have had with Stanley. Private my ass...our whole team remembered the specifics of the regional alignment discussions.

But my whole team wasn't impacted. My whole team wasn't the problem. I was.

So, the big Gold Circle reveal happened a couple of months later and, of course, my colleague won. As he is very aware of my crisis, he felt horrible. I explained to him to absolutely embrace the celebration because he had had a hell of a year and deserved to win just as much as I did. He should not feel guilty because he had nothing to do with what happened to me and, sincerely, I was thrilled for him. He was a great guy, who's also a wonderful husband and father, and who worked so hard that whole year. When I say he deserved to win, I meant it.

I ended up losing the #1 ranking by literally a few hundred dollars. To put that in perspective, we each carried a couple of million dollars in business. It was insane. I wanted to be able to just let it go but I couldn't. This situation was so unbelievably egregious.

With my colleague's knowledge and approval, I made one concentrated attempt to get Stanley and Don to correct what they had done by providing them and Operations with the exact numbers, dates, etc., of all of my orders related to my out-of-region clients and the revenue that was attached to them. It was to no avail. Based on the flippant congratulatory-omg-I've-never-seen-anything-like-this emails that were sent and comments that were repeatedly made on conference calls, Stanley and Don could barely contain themselves. I may have survived, and even succeeded in, the previous 10 months but they had showed me that they still had the power to inflict pain both financially and personally…and there wasn't a God damned thing I could do about it. I truly believe they felt they had won and that moment would be the final nail in the coffin. I'd have to quit now.

Funny thing about end games… Recognizing someone else's end game is incredibly important. However, as important as I have concluded that it is, as I mentioned before: I have found making sure I know and understand my own end game in every situation to be far more important. In fact, as previously mentioned, it may be the single most critical factor to my professional and personal success, as well as my overall happiness.

Winning Gold Circle wasn't my end game anymore than financial restitution was when my friend was asking me all those questions or keeping my job is now. Sure, losing Gold Circle sucked. But giving up or giving in at that point, especially then more than ever, knowing the lengths these people would continue to go to, was not an option. I had to stay in the fight. I had to stay pissed off. These people needed to be stopped. This type of behavior needed to stop. I needed to achieve my end game.

And now that they just added "REVENUE ALIGNMENT MODEL CHANGE WITH SINGULAR NEGATIVE IMPACT TO ONE PERSON" to my Harassment and Retaliation claim, they gave me even more ammunition to make that happen. I wasn't going anywhere.

Chapter 8
There's a Moment…

From childhood I have always been active in sports. I have probably at least tried them all at one point or another. I was good at some, not so good at others, but it didn't matter. I just always wanted to play, to test my endurance both physically and mentally. I imagine that thought sounds a bit too profound coming from a child, but it was true.

I happened to have been that annoying kid that was generally good at a lot of things. I always got excellent grades but never studied that hard. I could be in front of a room presenting or in a serious one-on-one with an adult and felt just as at ease as I did at the cafeteria lunch table. I could be taught a new sport or a new technique and grasp the gist of it without much effort, either, so I was always looking for a challenge. Something that wouldn't come easily. Something that I really had to work for which is why I think that I continually tried to learn different sports: if I had never done something before, there was a chance I'd have to work hard to get good.

My affinity to sports was a source of ambivalence in my household. On one hand, my parents loved that I was burning off all the boundless energy I seemed to have by participating in something constructive. On the other hand, with every new season came new waves of injuries, from getting spiked in the face with a volleyball that imbedded my brace-covered teeth into my lip to pulling my growth plate apart in my hip from running too much. If it was a weird, off-the-wall sort of injury, it seemed to find me. But I always took the injuries in stride just like I took all the practices between matches or meets or games or races, depending on what I happened to be into that season.

It was the work I craved so if I became injured, I just looked at it like something else I had to work through, not something devastating that I couldn't overcome. As I said, I was *that* annoying kid.

Probably my favorite, most enduring sport is long-distance running. Not because I was some nationally ranked standout with Olympic dreams, but because on any given run I needed just as much mental stamina as I did physical stamina and rarely were both of them readily available in equal force. A steep hill could try to fake out my mind or exhaust my legs. Bad weather could try to convince my mind it was too cold to run or my feet it was so slippery I could fall once I was outside. If I was studying I didn't have enough time to run. If I was running I probably should have been studying. It was like being on a teeter totter, but I loved it, constantly trying to push physical strength when I needed it and pull mental strength when I couldn't find any. After thirty years, that's a fact that holds true for me to this day. It's the epitome of an endurance test no matter what the distance.

One of the most fascinating aspects to me of my running mental-physical teeter totter is that no matter when I am running or where I am running or even if I am running against someone or all alone, there are always two pivotal moments: one where I don't think I am going to finish and contemplate stopping and another when I simply know that I am going to finish. Both are inevitable in my runner psyche. I never know if it's my mind or my body that is going to trigger either of them because the teeter totter is a fickle little contraption. But I do know they are going to happen. Not when, exactly, but I know. I know I am going to have this one moment of I-can't-possibly-keep-going and this other moment of I-absolutely-got-this. It's comforting in a fucked-up sort of way knowing that that inner turmoil is going to buddy up to me on my run. I never feel alone.

Since I once had a friend of my crisis say, "I told Stanley, if he's going to go after you, he better hope it's a sprint so he has a chance…because if it's a marathon, you'll beat anyone every time," I've wondered if there were pivotal moments during my crisis like there are during my runs. I have played that analogy out in my head over and over again these last few months.

And, as it turns out, there are.

In fact, the semblance of a really long run and my crisis is uncanny, eerie even. Peaks and valleys, headwinds and the wind at my back, cheering fans and alone with only my thoughts, sunshine and rainstorms…it's all there. The realization almost made me want to name my crisis "the marathon" until I remembered just how much respect I have for marathons.

I was driving home from a couple of states away when the first pivotal moment hit me. The one where I thought I was crumbling into a thousand pieces and could not go on. It was during that unstable January 2019, in the infancy of my crisis relatively speaking, but it was the moment that I not only realized that people were seriously on a mission to break me and to ruin my career, but also that other people who I cared about and respected deeply were getting caught in the crosshairs.

As I mentioned earlier, I would love to tell you that once I found strength in my breath or got into my pissed off state of mind that it was all rainbows and unicorns, but it wasn't. And, for that matter, it never will be. Even when we are strong, we falter. Even when we can control our breath at times, we feel like we are suffocating. Even when we are pissed off, we cry. The important thing that I have learned is to know in those desperate moments that I have a sanctuary of self to get back to. I may have to fight like hell to get back to it, but I know it is there and I know the way back…no matter how desolate the road I am on may seem. I have a map.

It was the day after I spent hours on the phone in those two dark parking lots--one call listening to Rachel telling me I was on my own and just needed to suck it up, and the other call listening to Theresa tell me about what happened to her and her colleagues, and how we had to fight for the future of her daughter. I had spent the night tossing and turning in my hotel bed, wrought with more emotions than I care to think about, let alone describe. I awoke from a fractured sleep and hoped that a light workout would clear my head enough to get through my morning meetings. When it didn't, I went straight to the caffeine steady drip of coffee, tea, those little 5-ounce energy shots…anything I could get my hands on because I was with Mimi that morning. I had to focus. More importantly, I had to be my A-Game on steroids and act like absolutely nothing was wrong.

Our morning went off without a hitch that I could see or sense. Mimi was happy. Clients were happy. I acted happy. All was perceptively right in the world.

Even when I began the long drive home, I remember feeling ok. Not great but not horrible. I remember it was a pretty, sunny day as I drove north on the highway. Then one of my in-the-know friends called to see how I was doing. It was the friend who made the "you better hope it's not a marathon" comment to Stanley so we were clearly close. I took the call.

We caught up as we often did. Yes, things still sucked. No, things weren't getting better. The particulars were standard even at such an early point in my crisis. But then somewhere between him telling me the shenanigans from his latest management conference call and me starting to tell him about my conversations with Rachel and Theresa the night before, the weight of the world came crashing down on me in my rental car. The worry, the stress, the tears all got caught in my throat and crippled my voice. My friend immediately heard the hitch in my voice and asked if I was ok.

As tears rolled down my cheeks, I told him that I couldn't believe what was happening to me, but even more so what was happening to other women who were involved. It wasn't fair that HR had called so many people in for such personal, invasive interviews and it was even less fair that Rachel had shared the content of those interviews with others who then used the information to inflict harm. I was devastated, feeling for the first time not that I was standing up for what was right, but rather that I had opened up pandora's box and it was swallowing me whole.

My friend talked to me as best he could, with sympathy for how exhausted and beat up I must have been feeling, and encouragement for my fight to change behaviors. He told me that none of my friends, him included, were worried about being questioned by HR or any senior leaders. They wanted to give me support. They wanted behaviors to change, too. He tried to get me to pull over to collect myself, but I just wanted to get home. I needed to get home to my dogs. I needed to get somewhere that I would feel safe.

He would later tell me that our phone call that day changed his perspective on my situation and how very bad things really were. It changed his perspective on working for our company. It was the first time he felt truly worried for me. And it was also when he officially decided to resign. He said that the cracks in my voice that day were heartbreaking to hear and convinced him that he couldn't keep working for the people who were deliberately causing someone he respected to feel that way.

After we ended our call, I still had about 100 miles to go. Plenty of time to cry. Plenty of miles to go a few rounds of What-Did-You-Get-Yourself-Into with myself. Plenty of time to start figuring out where I left my map so I could start heading back to good.

I remember replaying over and over again on that drive not just my conversations from the night before, but everything that had happened over the last handful of months. Fighting to get the over-charging issues addressed and taking the infamous HR call and building the now-defunct, inclusive Leadership Forum and fielding the accusations to me and my friends…all of it. All of the snarky tones and ambushing phone calls and epic emails detailing some new violation or frowned-upon behavior ran through my mind like they were on an old school movie reel, scene after scene.

By the time I pulled into my driveway, I was empty. Dehydrated from crying, exhausted from no sleep and a long drive. My brain was a puddle of goo. My brain had definitely triggered that first pivotal moment…that feeling that I could not keep going. Now I needed to figure out a way to get my body to start picking up the slack so my brain could regroup and eventually get back in the game.

The best way I know how to regroup when I am on a run that's falling apart is to slow down my breathing, lower my arm pumps and shorten my stride, but to *never stop moving*. I realize now that I applied the same principles that night: take focused, deep, long breaths, adjust my actions, but just keep moving. Since I couldn't change anything in my crisis at that moment, not to mention that my crisis seemed to have a death grip on me for the time being, I had to focus on something else I could impact. And I needed to make sure I got some serious sleep.

I took the time to make myself dinner so that I could do something I enjoyed as well as to get some healthy fuel in me. I wasn't hungry but I knew I needed to eat. If I didn't eat, it was going to be even a longer trip back to good. I then focused on my follow-up from the day's meetings. Since my follow-up always pertained to helping professionals better support their clients, my spirits immediately lifted a bit. Selfish as it may be, I needed those *feel-good feelings* from helping someone. Then, before I grabbed two Tylenol PM to make sure I would get a solid night's sleep, I started to clean the house. I could walk into a messy area, fix it, walk back out and not worry or simply know someone was going to walk in behind me and fuck it back up. It may sound silly but when everyone was either questioning what I was doing or undoing what I had already accomplished, even something as simple as an organized office or no dirty dishes in the sink felt good. I was moving.

Feeding myself, helping clients and their clients, cleaning my house and sleeping…that was my map back to good and back into the fight that night. Those were all concrete, positive behaviors that I could control immediately which is what I needed. I had felt so disempowered and helpless when I arrived home. I needed to control, or at least feel in control, of some aspects of my life. And since my brain was taking a much-needed hiatus after the last 24 hours of overload, my body stepped up, giving my brain some positive accomplishments to focus on once it was recharged. Again, silly as it sounds, finding something to hold onto, to pull myself back up, no matter how trivial, was my map. By the time I fell asleep, I wasn't 100% pissed off again and ready to fight but I was getting there.

When morning came and I realized I had slept a decent number of hours, I immediately felt more whole, less empty. Parts of the house were clean. I had good leftovers in the fridge. And I wasn't buried in work because I had completed much the night before. My accomplishments were all around me, insulating me from the shit that overwhelmed me the day before.

Nothing had changed except me. I was recharged. I was back in the fight. And I was really pissed off. Pissed off about everything that happened and pissed off because I let those bad actors steal even more of my energy, emotions and time than they already had. When my friend from the day before called to check in, I thanked him for listening to me and shared how I was feeling. I told him about my process the night before and we laughed about the next time I got that distraught I should farm out my services to my friends, offering to cook or clean at their homes. A side hustle born out of my crisis…that would be pretty funny. I thanked him again for caring and told him that I was not entirely ok but that I was getting my spirit back, my will to be in the fight was intact.

Little did I know that I would think back to that 24-hour period so often as the months went by, filled with more and more bizarre, retaliatory, harassing interactions. I did not yet know how much that empty feeling would stick with me as a barometer for future times when I thought I was breaking down or giving up. But then, because I had that January inflection point to pull from, realized I was in a tough moment but managing just fine. I also didn't know how often I would use that same standard map if I felt my control slipping—make food, help people, clean, sleep—or how much it would help me stay on course instead of falling astray.

Probably most interesting to me now is that I didn't have any idea how much my coping mechanisms to have a successful run, developed over many years and many miles, could translate into coping mechanisms to help me survive my crisis.

In the Summer of 2019, I had the second pivotal moment of my crisis: the one where I knew I was going to be ok. The one where I knew I was going to finish. Several weeks prior in April I reached out to an attorney that, coincidentally, I knew from previous work related to my company. She was extremely talented and knew a bit about my situation. Even though I assumed her taking my case would pose some conflict of interest, I hoped that she could recommend someone in her firm to me. She didn't disappoint.

I met with her and her colleague who would become my attorney in the middle of July 2019. I prepared for that meeting like it was the most important interview of my career. I compiled copies of all of my notes and chronicled emails and phone calls. I made copies of our Employee Handbook and Code of Conduct and Harassment Policies. I created a timeline of events stretching from Stanley describing me as "looking-good-in-a-skirt" years ago to the operations plans being altered to impact my performance. I needed him to know the only thing more serious than the situation I was facing was me.

And I was going to have one real shot to make him believe both.

See, in addition to preparing all my materials like my life depended on it, I also did research on my hopefully-soon-to-be attorney. Who was he and what was he about? I needed to know why my friend recommended him out of all of the attorneys she knew. One read of his bio, and I was sold.

Not only was he an active supporter of the #MeToo movement, but he also typically represented corporations *against* claims like mine. He was only going to take my case if it was legit and if he knew he'd have trouble representing the company if he were on the other side of the equation. He was exactly who I wanted representing me and my crisis. He would naturally be a skeptic.

We met for three hours and while at times he seemed to laugh at my over-preparedness, the laughter was not facetious. It was more pleasantly surprised in nature. He said he didn't typically get clients like me, where he had everything laid out for him with no initial work by his staff. Also, there weren't any evident holes or glaring red flags he had to consider which was unusual. I regarded those words as an invitation to keep going.

We walked through the timeline and the legend I made of cast members with their previous and current titles. We reviewed my notes and emails when he asked if I had proof of my claims. We talked and he took notes. And still we talked more. When we were wrapping up was when he told me two very critical points: first, I had enough data and proof to file multiple legitimate claims and, second, he was very interested in taking my case.

I was going to make it and this guy was going to help me.

The feeling of validation I had in that meeting room was indescribable. For months I had been documenting and recording and struggling to keep my head above water, all the while knowing in my gut what I was doing was right, but at times wondering if I was on a suicide mission because not even the most obviously basic bad behaviors were being condemned by my senior leadership or HR Department. And now, I sat across from these two extraordinarily experienced attorneys, one an expert in employment law and the other an expert in healthcare law, and both agreed that my case was solid and egregious from multiple angles. I turned internal cartwheels that day for me, for my friends, for the countless people who hadn't spoken up yet. I had found our first true advocate.

I left that appointment feeling hopeful…carefully guarded hope but definitely hope. I learned that not only had I maintained effective documentation and consistent behaviors, but also that when needed, I could recount my crisis without excessive emotion or breaking down. I had moments that I can only liken to what I have heard about what PTSD feels like, but I breathed through them. I felt strong. I felt supported. And I felt pissed off.

Interestingly, I went home and celebrated my milestone in a way surprisingly similar to when I nursed myself back from the brink that January night: I made an amazing meal, helped clients, cleaned the house and got some much-needed sleep. How weird. One situation I felt like my world was collapsing and the other I felt like my world was coming together. Why were my reactions identical?

As I stated in Chapter 1, I am in no way a therapist or psychologist or any other medical professional. My opinions and learnings and coping mechanisms are based purely on my life experiences of what has and hasn't worked, what I have seen, and what I realized about people long after many situations were over. And what I've concluded about coping mechanisms and celebration techniques during a crisis is this: sometimes they look exactly alike.

But why? Best as I can figure is that being human, my natural inclination is to go with what I know works. And my simple map—make food, help someone, clean the house, sleep—worked. It was easy and simple but made me feel a sense of accomplishment. It made my life better in small ways that carried over to the next day. And what I believe was most important, the behaviors in my map were incredibly normal during any point in my crisis since my current normal had been beyond fucked up for months. Whether driving home in January or leaving that law office in July, my day-to-day resembled nothing in my previous forty plus years on the earth. I needed as much normal as I could scrape together. So when I found that that set of behaviors created calm and made me feel somewhat like I did pre-crisis, it became a way for me to celebrate as much as a way for me to regroup and refocus. It became a way for me to remind myself that the old me was still there, supporting me in my crisis.

Chapter 9
Dogs, Attorneys & Interviews

One of the most incredible consequences of these last few months is the abundance of time I have spent with my rescue dogs. Like every other fur parent on the planet, I think my pups are the most *everything*: funny, adorable, playful, silly, cuddly, understanding…you name a way to humanize them, and I am likely a guilty party of it. However, there is one component of my pups that even if it is considered humanizing, I believe it to be an invaluable learning experience: how they communicate. It could be about how they are feeling or what they want. It could be where they want to go or what they want to do. They are nothing short of effective, as evident by the fact that they usually, eventually, get what they want. But why? And, more importantly, how?

See, my dogs listen to me for the most part. But they still get excited and jump a bit when they see someone for the first time. They still bark at the postal workers and God help any bunnies that get into my yard. But they're good dogs. They don't destroy anything. They don't whine or whimper for attention. And they are great travelers across the board. But they are, at the end of the day, still only dogs. They don't have any dog superpowers. They certainly can't talk. And yet they are two of the best negotiators I have ever went up against. They are relentless and patient and optimistic every time and in every way. I swear it's as if they can't fathom not getting what they want. That is simply how committed they are.

They have taught me more about communication and persuasion than any business book or seminar I have ever encountered. Most importantly, the skills they have taught me have shaped how I communicate with, of all people, attorneys—mine and, as I have recently learned, those that are charged with speaking to me in support of others' claims.

When my dogs communicate, regardless of what their current goal may be, they flawlessly execute with 3 simple actions and 1 simple reaction: eye contact, gentle persistence and patiently providing a comfortable amount of space so their focus person does not feel encroached upon...followed by gratefulness when they succeed. Whether I have a piece of grilled chicken on my plate or a new dog toy in my hand or I say their favorite two words on the planet—car ride—they never stray from their simple plan: I am going to look her in the eye and patiently follow her around at a reasonable distance, without barking or crying or jumping or anything, to let her know just how important what she has or wants to do is to me. And when I get what I want, I am going to be so tail-wagging, sloppy-kiss grateful that she is going to feel wonderful, too. The plan is brilliant in its simplicity. And, like I said, works just about every single time.

That's why I stole their plan.

If I replace "follow around at a reasonable distance" with "avoiding over-communicating via phone or email" and "barking and jumping" with "yelling and social media posts," I end up with a fairly clear-cut guide of how to effectively communicate with anyone who I want or need to work with, and lately those people are mostly attorneys. And, while I am certainly not planting grateful sloppy, wet kisses on anyone, I do trip over myself thanking everyone, anyone, for their time and consideration. When I look at my dogs' behaviors from that perspective, it's no wonder they are as successful as they are.

Of course my crisis, even on my best days, is a constant part of my existence, but it is only one of many cases to my attorney, a reminder I have to often give myself. He has dozens of other cases covering a vast array of topics and issues with just as many personalities and end games involved. He is busy and I respect that…I even prefer that because who really wants an attorney with tons of free time available to represent them? Not me.

Where his case load changes from being impressive to a pain point for me is when I believe I *need* to speak to him because of something I have deemed critically important to know or share with him now…*like right now*…and he's not available and sometimes can't be available for days. Why I have determined this one thing or that one point to be so urgent varies on the situation. At times in retrospect I laugh because I realize I tried to kidnap myself into the emotional hijacking van for absolutely no good reason. I mean, it's not as though anything I would get to tell him or question I would get answered is going to change anything I am going to do: I am on forced leave in the middle of a drawn out legal situation during a pandemic…I am not going anywhere or, for all practical purposes, going to do anything. But, at the end of the day, many times I still want to have that interaction or that knowledge so instead of throwing myself into my own van, I tap into 2 of my key dog learnings: patient persistence without overcrowding.

I think carefully about what I need and why, determining if I really need something versus just wanting something to happen. I choose my words cautiously to form the most concise, professional message possible. Then I choose the best mode of communication: text, phone, or email, because I am only using one. I can't go all needy girlfriend and pull a did-you-see-my-email text, if he doesn't respond to the email, followed by a call in case, you know, he didn't see my text, either. Not a good strategy to get a call back from anyone, least of all my busy attorney. I have to be smart. I have to follow a plan. I have to be patient. I typically give him 3-5 days to respond, and I must say, more than a year into our situation together, while at times I truly struggle with my restraint, the plan works a good amount of the time. I think, in fact *I know*, it would be even more effective if I could somehow in a non-creepy way factor the constant eye contact into those electronic message methods, but I'll work with what I got for now.

These exercises in patience and being ok with not knowing everything all the time have helped me for the times where we really do need to talk, too. Those times are serious and important, often fairly calculated in content and purpose and time. I recognize that these moments don't come often so I approach scheduling and participating in those meetings with that same focus: eye contact, patient persistence, no over-crowding and gratefulness. I come prepared with my list of need-to-knows written out so I can avoid unnecessary follow-up communications and embarrassing missteps. I rarely break eye contact when we are in-person or on a ZOOM and always follow-up with a verbal thank you before I leave and a written thank you after I've gone. My efforts may sound like overkill, but we are finally in the vicinity of the finish line, and I don't think either of us—attorney or client—are taking the other one for granted. I call that a win.

I believe as much as this simple plan has benefitted my dogs with treats and car rides over the years, it has also clearly benefitted me in far more serious, life-changing ways thus far in my crisis…first, with my own attorney and more recently with the formal investigation that my company launched, using a high-powered, external law firm.

Yep, that finally happened…23 months after I first reported serious concerns, 10 months after I filed with the EEOC, and nearly 6 months after I was placed on leave. Go figure.

A few weeks ago my attorney notified me that my company had hired this external law firm to investigate my claims. We weren't initially clear on what aspect of my situation they would be investigating or who they would be talking to, but I quickly learned from a friend who was interviewed that the scope was to be limited to my EEOC charges. "Someone else" internally is investigating my other concerns, whatever that means.

When the external attorney first reached out to my attorney, he was a bit of a douche, stating I wasn't permitted to have legal counsel present because it was an internal investigation and I had to turn over all my "proof" to him. My attorney quickly squelched those ideas with a commonsense response that included, quite simply, that the time for an internal investigation was probably in 2018 or 2019 when I originally brought concerns to senior leadership…not in late Summer of 2020 after I had filed formal charges and been on forced leave for several months. Guess the guy had to give it a try, though.

The original 2-hour requested interview time became 4 hours over 2 days. It really was more interesting than exhausting, more liberating than stressful. When I reflect upon the interactions, they seem to compartmentalize in my mind the same way any presentations I have given do: Was it work? Yes. Was it difficult? No. Was I nervous? No. I never present on something I don't know like the back of my hand. I always say "I don't know" when I don't know, rather than giving some long, idiotic rationalization that ends up making me look like a lying, nervous fool. And I always look my audience in the eye, clarify any questions they have, and thank them when I am finished.

Yes, these interviews were *exactly* like my presentations.

The fact-finding attorney, as he called himself, ended up being a reasonable, pleasant guy. I learned he was going through my submitted EEOC case line-by-line to verify the accuracy of what was included, corroborate the details with any names that were provided, and obtain any related materials that could serve as hard proof. I remember thinking and laughing to myself as he began, "I don't know what this guy is used to as far as proof, but maybe I should just tell him to check that box next to every line item we are going to cover to save both of us some time."

As I have recounted to my trust-tree of friends, for the most part the interview went as you would expect—he asked questions, I answered them, rinse, repeat. He was never contentious or assuming or accusing. He genuinely presented himself as seeking to understand and to capture the truth as I knew it to be. But I must admit, there were a few moments that I found incredibly validating, fucking hilarious or some combination of both. And it's during those particular moments…those moments where I either wanted to burst out laughing or make some smug, I-can't-make-this-shit-up response…that I truly had to ignite my inner dog teachings: eye contact, patience, and space.

One of those moments occurred when he recounted details from an incident in the Winter of 2017 that I previously shared. This was the incident, as you may recall, where I confronted Stanley in front of his boss, Don, about the negative remarks he made about me to my colleague and his sales rep. The attorney, in rereading the EEOC entry to me, misread the statement. Actually, when he said it to me, he said it correctly. When he internalized it to ask me a question, it came out backwards…or, as any businesswoman will attest to, it came out as a standard society stereotype or assumption. It came out as he believed it should be based on *his* life perspective.

Eye contact, patience, space…and definitely no laughing.

What he read to me went like this:

"…Stanley stated things got emotional and that's why he said the comments that he did about you."

But when he asked me questions about the entry, it went like this:

The attorney offered up, "So, at what point were you told you were being emotional? And, who stated that you were being emotional, Stanley or Don?"

A pause…then a breath…then I replied, "Respectfully, I am not sure if there is a typo on your copy or if maybe you misspoke, but no one told me I was being emotional. Stanley stated that he was emotional the day he made the comments about me and that is what caused him to make the comments he made."

Confused, the attorney asked, "Oh, so you weren't accused of being emotional?"

Perhaps a little-too-strong, "No" was my response.

The attorney seemed to be gathering himself, and when he did asked with what I would call trepidation, "And Stanley stated that he was emotional AND that he made those comments about you?"

"Yes," I replied. How much more clarification do we need?

Well, apparently at least a little more based on the attorney asking, "He admitted making them?"

Another big ol' "Yes" here, my friend.

The attorney persisted with, "Did he tell you what he was emotional about that day?"

I replied with a simple, "No. I didn't ask. I didn't think it mattered."

And then it happened…the attorney asked, "Did you respond in any way?" And the heavens of speech opened up and allowed me to answer, "Yes. I asked him to be less emotional at work in the future and to stop talking about me behind my back."

Women everywhere, alive and passed, at-home executives and in-office executives, younger and older and anywhere in between, newbies and those with lifetimes of experience, all stood up in that moment and said, "I know that's right" in unison.

For the gentlemen that have been interested enough to read this far, I thank you, but I also sincerely mean when I say that you truly can't understand the power in that moment, whether in 2017 when it originally happened or in 2020 when it was awkwardly recounted between me and an attorney. All women…*any woman*…no matter what they do or where they are from, are more frequently than not assumed from the get to be emotional. We can even react exactly the same way as a male counterpart does *at the same time*, and he is impassioned and reached his breaking point of tolerance and we, more often than not, have over-reacted, become hysterical and lost our minds. Every woman that has thankfully chosen to read this far can provide a personal example that has happened to her. If you don't believe me, simply ask any woman that you know. She will tell you. I promise. Just keep in mind: you should never ask a question that you don't want to hear the answer to…in other words, if her answer involves *you*, embrace the suck and learn, my friend. Embrace the suck and learn.

Another pivotal moment occurred at the end of the first day of my interview. We were running out of the allotted time and deciding on when to reconvene the next day. While I was in the middle of thanking the external attorney, and my attorney, for their time and consideration, I called an internal audible. I believed up until that point I had represented myself authentically and without pretense, but I wanted to end the day on unquestionable solid footing. So I rolled the dice, and it went like this:

"Before we end for the day, I want to make sure that you understand I never wanted to be here. I never wanted things to get to this point and I did everything in my power to avoid it. Every time you've asked me if I have proof or emails or notes, I have said, "Yes." And every time I have replied, "Yes," I have personally referenced this bound notebook that I am now holding up in front of the camera. For 4 years I have kept real-time notes on everything that's happened to me. They're in this notebook that can't have pages added to it and anyone could see if I have taken any pages away. I have offered the pages in this notebook at least half a dozen times, as documented within the notebook entries, to Compliance, HR and multiple senior leaders at my company for years, and no one ever wanted to look at it. They all outwardly declined my offers. I have no idea why, but they did. Had any one of them accepted, I believe these issues could have been addressed and we wouldn't be here."

I try to avoid over-interpreting someone's facial expressions or dissecting responses or lack thereof, but I genuinely feel he was gob smacked. His only response was:

"Well, I would definitely like to see your notebook."

All that came to my mind was, *I bet you would.* Even with a couple weeks having passed since then, I can't help but wonder what he was thinking in that moment. Did he think that his job just became a hell of a lot easier or more difficult? Did he wonder how he was going to tell my company's head legal counsel that had any one of half a dozen people simply taken my notebook and given it to him, they wouldn't be in this clusterfuck of a situation? Or did he just have an internal giggle at all publicly traded companies for helping him create such a successful career for himself out of their own arrogance and ignorance? I'll never know but I do know when we began the next day, he had follow-up questions, not to my answers given the day before, but to my notebook, so it had obviously been on his mind since we last talked.

Are there any copies? Yes.

Did I keep notes in real-time or as I remembered to input them? Real-time.

Would we provide him with my notes? Absolutely, if my attorney approves.

I just shake my head thinking about all of it now, which leads me to the final interview moment that I believe is worth mentioning to you.

Please know I don't mean to imply that there weren't other interactions during my interview that caused me to pause or wonder or laugh or just say how-did-I-end-up-here, but most of those are probably only interesting to me and a few select people. This last moment, though, I feel is not only a universal you-can't-be-serious moment, but also a moment where I activated every effective, dog-based tactic I ever learned: eye contact, patience, persistence, space, follow-thru, urgency, gratefulness. Add into those dog-learnings the importance I'd come to place on breathing through situations for strength and pulling from prior experiences for perspective and I had the quintessential this-is-what-I-have-been-training-for moment of all moments. All at once, after the cathartic experience of the previous 4 hours of interviews, feeling as though I was finally being heard by an impartial party who would act, reality came crashing back down on my head like a ton of bricks with two sentences:

"Anslie, thank you so much for your time and willingness to speak to me. This concludes my inquiry as the last entry for the EEOC charge I have was what we just covered in the Winter of 2019 until your administrative leave in the early Spring of 2020."

I'm sorry…excuse me…I beg your pardon…and any other what-the-fuck pause you can think of…but are you serious? That's what went through my head. Fortunately, what came out of my mouth, went like this:

"I'm sorry, but if we could take a few more minutes, I need to ask: Are you saying that your understanding is that after the Winter incident that we just discussed, everything was fine and then I was suddenly placed on leave in the Spring of 2020?"

The attorney replied, "Yes. That's what I have."

The only thing that kept my feelings from blocking my throat was that breath…just breathe. As calmly as I could, I shared, "That's not exactly true. In fact, it's not true at all."

The attorney replied with a mix of confusion and fatigue with, "Was there more that happened?"

"Why, yes, there was. Did you not receive a copy of the email I sent to the head of our legal department and the head of our HR department a few months ago?" At this point my breath and heart and emotions were fighting for space in my throat and no one was winning.

Then an eerie calm came over the attorney and he stated, "No. I have no idea what you're talking about." And then he just stared. Stared a hole through that ZOOM screen right into me.

I took a deeper breath and replied:

"Well, it's something that I believe is important. For about six weeks after I filed the EEOC charges and after the Winter incidents, the people involved essentially froze me out. I think, not that you care or can comment, but I think it was meant to make me feel isolated, but I actually felt free to do my job for the first time in ages. But then a couple of months later, the people involved across the board in my situation picked up their harassing and retaliatory and misogynistic behaviors to the degree that they had in previous months. With the consent of my attorney, I submitted to the heads of Legal and HR at my company a detailed timeline of events and interactions that transpired since my EEOC filing, telling them that despite my EEOC filing, my situation continued to deteriorate. Less than 2 weeks later, without notice, I was placed on forced administrative leave. Since then, the people I have accused of wrongdoings are working and receiving paychecks and going about their lives, while I have gone from a forced, paid administrative leave to a forced, unpaid administrative leave, to a leave that is now about to also stop my insurance coverage, causing employees and clients to question where I am and what I have done."

I watched the attorney take a deep breath and heard him say, "Do you have a copy of that email?"

"Of course, I do" was all I could say at that point.

And then I swear I watched him on screen regroup and refocus himself right before he said, "If you could include that in what you send me, that would be very helpful."

I can't remember my exact response but it resembled, "Yeah, that won't be a problem."

In that moment I naively realized that my company's "independent, external investigation," was only as independent as they wanted it to be. What other critical information had they not afforded this investigator? What other data points had they shaded to the exact colors that matched their end game? I should have known…really, it should not have surprised me, but it did, nonetheless. I had been professionally seduced by an "Independent" party listening to me. I thought the difference and the change I had been lamenting over for the last few years was finally on the cusp of happening. While it was, it also wasn't. I was still in the fight, and I still had work to do.

This was truly a life-pausing moment for me. Not just in my crisis, but in the grander scheme of my life as a whole…I will permanently remember it for as long as I can remember anything. I will also remember the moments that followed where I breathed…where I knew I had the data to back up everything I had said…where I knew the people I had referenced would speak out and stand up in the truths of what happened…where I knew not only I would be ok, but also that this situation…*my crisis*…would be the new, different, stronger foundation of what was next for me and, probably of equal importance, what was next for so many of the people I cared about.

Chapter 10
What's Next?

At least once I think everyone hears a version of the quote "the truth is a funny thing" at some point in their life. They likely hear it a lot more than once and probably have had their own personal experience where they've said it themselves after a particular situation. I have found myself saying it quite a bit over these last few years, and even more over these last several months of my life. I say it to myself. I say it to my dogs. I say it to my close friends who are not personally involved in my crisis but who have listened, sometimes incredulously, to the details. I say it to my friends and colleagues who have been questioned by leadership, audited by Compliance and interviewed by external counsel. I say it to my attorney, and even the assigned mediator, when I am describing interactions and experiences and they ask clarifying questions, thinking maybe I misspoke or overstated or simply inferred a feeling rather than someone having directly said or done something to me.

The truth is a funny thing…*sometimes a really funny thing*.

Granted, truth is often not heard or realized in the timeframe that we would like it to be because we all want to be heard now. Yesterday. Sooner definitely not later. Especially if we are being wronged or hurt in some way. But that's not how life works out. Life works out the way it's supposed to and truths are part of that process...*eventually*.

As soon as I accepted that fact, the fact that I can only continue to speak the truth but cannot control people hearing or acting on it, my overall being improved exponentially. In fact, as soon as I realized I couldn't really control anything or anyone outside of myself, internally I became an eerie sort of calm that is hard for me to explain to others, even those closest to me. A calm that is confident but humble and strong but vulnerable all at once. I would almost liken it to a feeling of freedom once I realized what I had absolute control over, that being myself, and what I had absolutely no control over, which is anything outside of my own truths. At this late point in my crisis this realization has led me to what might sound like a daunting question:

What's next?

By the time anyone reads this, I will be on the other side of my crisis, getting to know *the other side me*. But right now, as I sit here in the early morning on my couch in my favorite quarantine wide-leg sweatpants, drinking coffee out of my favorite oversized mug, I only have a vague idea. A notion of what's next. Some plans but not a master plan...and that's ok because that's how it must be right now. And *that* is ok because I continue to have a blind faith in where my truth is leading me next. Remember...it's one of the only things I can control. Much like I only have so much RAM, I now know I only have so much control, and it has taken my crisis to teach me that life lesson. Let me explain.

Countless times over the last few years people, both men and women, have told me they don't know how I am "doing it" or surviving or seeming to thrive. Or, in a retrospective fashion will comment on their astonishment at the strength they perceive me to have possessed in this situation or in that moment. We talked about this in earlier pages. We talked about breathing and strength and selfishness and being pissed off…all of which are my truths of surviving and growing through my crisis. All of which got me here. But the one truth I haven't mentioned until now that has been crucial throughout my crisis and will continue to be invaluable long after it and its cast members are in my rearview mirror, is learning to relinquish the fantasy control I thought I should have, or needed to have, over anything in my life except myself. At the risk of sounding like a motivational poster about attitude in a corporate office or an affirmation from some inspirational speaker, *that* truth has set me free. I'm controlling what I can control. I am the master of my domain. No one can fuck with my chi. Yeah, all that stuff.

But it's true. Outside of always speaking the truth at any cost throughout my crisis, and controlling my actions and reactions, I have had no control over anything else that has happened. Sure, I have attempted to influence perspectives and sometimes it has worked…I think. And I have certainly counseled different people and given tons of presentations that I suppose had an impact…I think. But, at the end of the day, who really knows? Was I really that influential or that impactful or were people just giving me lip service, saying what they thought they should say to appear to be open-minded or a change agent or a sympathizer? Not only do I not know, but I will likely never know. And again…that's ok. Because all of those energies and thoughts and strategic plans I used to waste on the what-ifs of others, I have repurposed into myself and in doing so, have become very intrigued, and even inspired again, in the unknowns of what is next for me. As I shared earlier, and trust me when I say it now, learning how to be ok with being selfish when I need to be may be one of the most important changes I have ever personally made. And investing those energies in myself? Well, that's a type of selfish I can get used to.

So, let's see, as far as what is next, what do I know on this Day 186 of my leave? Well, I know that in less than 10 days we are to sit down for another mediation. People have asked me how I am feeling about it, if the fact a formal investigation has occurred or that more time has passed, has changed my mind in any way. Most of the time I answer I don't feel one way or the other about it and most of the time that answer is accurate. Sometimes I get excited and caught up daydreaming about this finally being over and what changes are going to be made and how the company's culture might change and what I can create to help other women who understandably can't fathom blowing up their own lives to fight a serious, systemic wrong no matter how much suffering that wrong is causing them and others. At other, more rare moments my breath will get caught in my throat or I'll lay awake staring at the ceiling because it hits me that I did blow up my life and realize I don't know what is going to happen. I can only hope. It's in those moments, though, that I feel that freedom and peace wash over me, knowing that I can only control myself, and, since I believe in myself more than I believe in anything else, I know that I am going to soar into the mostly unknown next phase of my life.

I say *mostly unknown* because, come on, I may have become a Type A Hippie over these last several months, but Type A is Type A. I've been getting a bit more done than gardening, making candles and hiking…I've just been going about it quietly.

Once my company stopped paying me during the administrative leave, I told my attorney that I felt that action limited what they could tell me to do or not do moving forward. Kind of in the same vein I have told my friends over the years that if they want their parents to stop feeling entitled to interfere in their lives or dictate their decisions, stop taking their money. It's pretty simple: if you are self-funding, you have the right to make your own independent decisions. People can complain, but they can't do a damn thing about it.

So, I let my attorney know that I wanted to consult. I had previous clients who were interested in the services I could provide, and they were willing to pay for it. Common sense told me that I'd have to steer clear of anything related to my company's business, or that of their competitors, which was fine by me. And I guessed I'd have to maintain the confidentiality of the situation I was in which wouldn't be a problem since I didn't want to try to explain all of the craziness to anyone anyway. I thought this was an easy ask. But, again, I can't control anything outside of myself so of course it wasn't that easy.

After my attorney's initial request to my company's Employment attorney…as I told you, there are a lot of attorneys in my orbit these days…it took them weeks to respond, and the response was ridiculous. Sure, I could consult and, of course, it included the non-compete and privacy factors I mentioned in the last paragraph. But they added their own spice to it: In order to consult, I would have to submit to HR who I was consulting with and what the scope of my purpose was so they could decide whether or not there was a conflict of interest.

Fuck that nonsense.

So I was to what? Submit a business case to them about internal projects that CEOs wanted me to run to fix things in their companies that they likely didn't want others to know existed? Yeah, that wasn't about to happen. I mean, Jesus, what if they called the customer to verify anything? That was a whole new level of awkward I needed to avoid experiencing.

I gave myself a couple of days to feel defeated, have a few cocktails and just generally stew in the momentary stagnant point of my crisis. Shit, there was a pandemic going on so it's not like staying home was any noticeable activity…and then I got back to being effectively pissed off and wrote a letter to the VP of HR at my company. I explained my understanding of and respect for both the process we were in and the parameters that were set forth. I laid out the general context of what I wanted to do and emphasized that it in no way hinted towards anything conflicting or inappropriate in nature. And I expressed that sharing specific details on clients, their locations and the scope of my work in each location seemed unnecessary.

My attorney sent it and a couple of weeks later I was granted permission. I didn't even care that they dragged their feet. I could become a contributing member of society again, albeit a modest one and I was thrilled. For all practical purposes, until my situation resolved, I'd be limited to working with people who either knew something about my situation already or knew me well enough to know that whatever was going on behind the scenes was not detrimental to them in any way or I wouldn't be talking to them. I could work with this.

In the midst of my newfound excitement, I did hit a minor but really not so minor speed bump. Oh, who am I kidding? I momentarily lost my mind. I dove into the fucking van. My friend Christopher pulled a rare, rapid sequence of Face Timing me, texting me when I didn't answer and calling me when I didn't respond. It made me laugh because he was acting so Stanley-like which he abhorred, but then I wondered if something was really wrong. When we got on the phone and I confirmed he wasn't dying, he insisted that I FaceTime him immediately. Ok, this was officially weird.

As soon as our phones connected, he faced the camera to his computer screen and asked if I could see it. Sure, I could, but why was I looking at an Outlook calendar and who's calendar was it? That's when he zoomed in and it became clear as day: on Stanley's public calendar, available for anyone to see or screenshot, nestled amidst 4 other appointments labeled as "private", was a public appointment listed…with the name "Krewicco" and the word "litigation" right in the subject heading.

Anyone could see it. Anyone could take a picture and show, well, anyone. I am the only person with that last name in the whole company. I lost my mind.

There I was maintaining every aspect of privacy and decorum that was expected of me in this entire process…this process that they requested to keep things out of the public eye …and then this fucktard Stanley puts a god damned billboard on his Outlook calendar. Who knows who saw it or who they shared that little nugget with outside of the company. What if any of my clients or prospects found out? Jesus Christ.

I took a few minutes to stop the van, put it in park and walk away from it before I called my attorney. Dog learnings, breathing, controlling myself…at that point in time, I was probably pulling from things I didn't even know about so I wouldn't sound like a crazy person to my attorney. When I got his voicemail, I left a very even-toned message. I told him what happened, what it immediately meant, what it could possibly mean and that he needed to get the calendar entry removed as soon as humanly possible. As I continued to find calm, I realized that ultimately it only helped prove my point of Stanley's retaliation and harassing behavior. I wish it hadn't happened, but at least there was a silver lining I could envision.

It took more than a few days for Stanley's calendar to become privatized which was a bit aggravating but, again, I knew it would all be fine and was actually helping in a back-handed sort of way. I learned that up until the mediator finally had to force my company back to the table a couple of weeks after that incident, they had been non-responsive for the previous several weeks, so I am sure the calendar entry fiasco didn't help whatever entanglement they suddenly found themselves in internally. I didn't feel at all bad or even personally worried a bit, but it did make me a little curious. I wondered what realities were they finally being forced to deal with and, even more curious, *how* were they planning to deal with them? I know it's another uncontrollable that I am unable to know right now, but it's one of the ones that I don't mind wasting some time thinking about every so often. I mean, really, shit had to get real and quick.

The calendar entry situation passed, and they apologized and claimed, "dumb oversight," which even the mediator knew was bullshit, but after I said my peace, I let it go. The underlying point had been made to them: they had bad actors that were still negatively impacting my life on the leave they forced me to take…and I was the one that gave them the proof…again. There wasn't anything left to do but to get back to figuring out how I want to approach my new professional adventure while I wait for the next phase of my crisis to come.

After a few weeks of creative development and reaching out to specific clients, I understood that I really had more than kind-of-a-good-idea on my hands. I always thought my concept would receive a positive response, but I had remained cautiously optimistic. People were interested and what I was offering was different, so different that I had one contract signed immediately to begin a project and another contract signed with a vendor partner for us to share leads and create focused network events. I was about to start having fun again.

To protect myself, I went through the process of creating an LLC and learned all the boring but important aspects of actually being self-employed. I designed and ordered business cards, flushed out my value proposition and even got my accounting practices set up. I sought advice and feedback from people I trust and became the learner sponge again that I've been my entire life. I know I can't turn all of the lights on for a while, but the moment I can, my "Type A" ass will be ready.

I will hopefully have a few independent projects under my belt and a few more in progress when I can turn the lights on, so my go-live date will be more of an exhilarating, exhaled, "Now…it's time," rather than a nervous, holding-my-breath, "Wow…it's really that time."

I am almost as excited at the prospect of doing my own thing as I am at putting my crisis behind me and simply using the learnings from it as a new foundation to stand on. What I am most intrigued by is that I know there is so much that I don't know and that I still have to learn. You can't imagine how simply overwhelming and amazing it is to feel that way, to be inspired in that way…not just after the last few years, but also in spite of the fact that my crisis is still very much alive and a part of my life. We are not done yet. I am still in the fight. But in breathing this rare air, I know whatever is next will be like nothing I have ever experienced before. There is a new me now that didn't exist before my crisis just like there will be another new me on the other side of it…and I cannot wait to meet her.

Rare Air

When I started writing this book several weeks ago, I had an idea of where it would go and the story it would tell, but I didn't realize the journey it would take me on personally. I wasn't expecting there to be many, if any, surprises. I was wrong. By not simply recounting the details but including what I was thinking during those moments has been beyond cathartic and, at the risk of sounding cliché, given me a new perspective on my crisis and the life I am leading now. So many of the instances I detailed I have thought about too many times to count, but maybe never realized how much I was growing or didn't value their importance or didn't know how much I would rely on them moving forward. I definitely didn't realize all of the beauty and positives that came out of so much emotional devastation and professional struggle. But it was there the whole time. I just needed the space...*the rare air*...to realize it.

As I said when we began, this rare air never happens until it does, and you certainly have to be lucky enough to be aware that it's happening when it does, or it will pass you by without even a nudge. But I do believe that I have the control to create pockets of it in the future so that I can reflect and learn and grow more in real time during conflicting times or moments of pain…and so do you. How incredible would it have been to recognize sooner all of these things I now know I've learned? How would have I handled my crisis differently? When I ask myself questions like those, I realize that making time to breathe or to be selfish or to be pissed off while I am seemingly in challenging moments is going to be a non-negotiable for me moving forward. It simply must be. The value of taking those moments has been undeniable to me in coping with and accepting my crisis and will continue to be crucial to my happiness after I have moved passed it. We all deserve to take an extra five minutes and I promise you, unless you're a surgeon or a hostage negotiator or a bomb expert or some other critical frontline, first responder, you cannot possibly invest those five minutes in anything better than yourself.

As I wonder how my crisis will conclude over these next few weeks, I am filled with an inner calm and happiness, regardless of the outcome and regardless if it drags out longer. I am not worried. I am not afraid. On the contrary, I am filled with hope at this next unknown, this next adventure…

For *the new me…the new Anslie…*

Inhale…exhale…repeat.

About the Author

Nicole/Rowin was born in Beaver Falls, PA, but has resided in Ohio her entire adult life. She has spent much of her career in the healthcare arena and launched her own consulting company in 2020. She is known for being open-minded but decisive, with a commitment to compassion, equity and working diligently to give a voice to people who have either lost their own voice or never knew they had one in the first place. When she's not traveling around the country improving access for patients to receive care or teaching leadership seminars, she can be found renovating her house or hiking with her 2 rescue dogs.

* 9 7 9 8 2 1 8 1 3 3 6 0 3 *